W9-AYM-603

DEMON IN MY VIEW

9/04

ᴀᴍᴇʟɪᴀ ᴀᴛᴡᴀᴛᴇʀ-ʀʜᴏᴅᴇꜱ

ISBN: 0-440-22884-0

RL: 6.0

Reprinted by arrangement with Delacorte Press

Printed in the United States of America

September 2001

10 9 8 7 6 5

OPM

Dedicated to Jessica Guenther, who is a pillar of strength in rough times, an inspiration, and one of Aubrey's greatest admirers.

Thanks also to everyone who has helped me:

Sarah Lancaster, Sara Keleher, Andrea Brodeur, and Carolyn Barnes for their support and friendship, my sister Rachel for hours of work looking through poetry, Rick Ballard and Steve Wengrovitz for their help editing, and Natasha Rorrer and Nathan Plummer for listening patiently to all my complaints and offering their suggestions. To anyone I missed, thank you. I never could have done this without you.

Alone

From childhood's hour I have not been
As others were—I have not seen
As others saw—I could not bring
My passions from a common spring—
From the same source I have not taken
My sorrow—I could not awaken
My heart to joy at the same tone—
And all I lov'd—*I* lov'd alone—
Then—in my childhood—in the dawn
Of a most stormy life—was drawn
From ev'ry depth of good and ill
The mystery which binds me still—
From the torrent, or the fountain—
From the red cliff of the mountain—
From the sun that round me roll'd
In its autumn tint of gold—
From the lighting of the sky
As it pass'd me flying by—
From the thunder, and the storm—
And the cloud that took the form
(When the rest of Heaven was blue)
Of a demon in my view—

Edgar Allan Poe

PROLOGUE

THE NIGHT IS FULL OF MYSTERY. Even when the moon is brightest, secrets hide everywhere. Then the sun rises and its rays cast so many shadows that the day creates more illusion than all the veiled truth of the night.

I have lived in this illusion for much of my life, but I have never belonged to it. Before my birth, I existed for too long in the realm between nothingness and life, and even now, the night still whispers to me. A strong cord binds me to the dark side of the world, and shields me from the light.

CHAPTER I

THE BLACK OBLIVION OF SLEEP was shattered by the caterwauling of some singer on Jessica's clock radio. She groaned and viciously beat the alarm clock into silence, then groped blindly for the light switch. The somber red glow of her Lava lamp provided just enough light to read the time.

Seven o'clock. The red numbers glowed sadistically, and Jessica swore. Only two hours of sleep again. How she managed to remain in the conscious world at all was a mystery, but she dragged herself into the shower, where the cold water finished what the alarm clock had started.

Only one hundred and eighty days of school left,

Jessica thought as she prepared for the first day of her senior year of high school. There was barely enough time to get dressed before she had to pull her backpack onto her shoulders and dart down the street to catch the bus. Breakfast? A fleeting dream.

Ah, Ramsa High School. What a perfect little niche of Hell, she thought as the bus pulled up to the school. *In one year, you will be out of here forever.* That fact was the only thing that had convinced Jessica to get out of bed that morning: if she passed senior year, she would never need to succumb to the grasp of Ramsa High again.

She had lived in the town of Ramsa since she was twelve, and had long before realized that the other students would never accept her. Few were openly hostile, but no one could be described as warm and fuzzy, either.

As she neared the building, Jessica was acutely aware of how many students walked in groups of friends. She had known these people for five years, but that didn't seem to matter as they moved past her without a word. She even saw two girls notice her, whisper to each other, then quickly retreat as if Jessica was somehow dangerous.

One senior, a boy Jessica had known since her very first day at Ramsa Junior High, crossed himself when he saw her. She was tempted to start chanting satanically in the hopes of scaring him. He had long before decided that she must be a witch, and she had no idea why. Occasionally, out of spite or simply boredom, she encouraged his belief.

The thought was amusing in a way. The only witches she knew lived solely in the confines of the novels she'd been writing for the past few years. One of her witches could walk right in front of this idiot and he would never recognize her as what she was; Jessica's witches tended to be rather human in their manner and appearance.

More humorous, though, was the fact that her old enemy was holding the book *Tiger, Tiger* by Ash Night. Jessica wondered how he would react if he knew that she would soon be receiving royalties from his purchase.

Jessica had been struck by the idea for *Tiger, Tiger* several years before, when she and Anne had been visiting one of Anne's old college friends in Concord, Massachusetts. She had spent nearly the entire week-end vacation locked in her room, and those hours of work had finally paid off.

In homeroom, Jessica sat in the back, alone as always. She waited in silent contemplation for attendance to be taken. The teacher was a young woman whom Jessica had not seen before; her name was written on the board and had received a few snickers from the students. Kate Katherine, high-school teacher, must have had sick parents. On the other hand, her name was probably easier for people to remember than Jessica Ashley Allodola.

"Jessica Allodola?" Mrs. Katherine said as if cued by Jessica's thoughts.

"Here," Jessica answered absently. The teacher checked off the name in her book and went on to the next person on the list.

The words of Jessica's adoptive mother, Anne, echoed through her mind.

"Tomorrow is the first day of a new year, Jessie. Could you at least try not to get sent to the office? Just this once?"

"Don't call me Jessie," she had answered.

"Just try, Jessica," Anne had pleaded. *"For me?"*

"You aren't my mother. Don't tell me what to do."

"I'm the closest thing to a mother you have!" Anne had snarled, losing her patience.

The remark had stung, and Jessica had stalked to her room, mumbling, *"My* real *mother was smart enough to get rid of me early."*

Snapping back to the present, she wondered bitterly if Anne considered it bad luck that Jessica was the child she had ended up adopting. Jessica wrenched herself from these thoughts as a pretty girl with chestnut hair tentatively entered the room.

"I'm sorry I'm late," the girl said. "I'm new to the school, and I got a bit lost." She introduced herself as Caryn Rashida. Mrs. Katherine nodded as she found Caryn's name on her list.

Caryn looked around for an empty seat; one was conveniently located next to Jessica. But when she saw Jessica she hesitated, as if she might go sit somewhere else. Jessica wasn't surprised. The residents of Ramsa all seemed to shy away from her almost unconsciously.

However, Caryn made up her mind and walked resolutely across the room. Extending a hand, she spoke. "Hi. I'm Caryn Rashida." She stumbled a bit over her own last name. "Why are you sitting all alone here?"

" 'Cause I want to," Jessica answered coolly, leveling her emerald-green eyes at Caryn's pale blue ones. Caryn held the gaze for a moment longer than most people could, but then looked away.

With disgust, Jessica had noted the girl's unease and her decision to make an effort despite it. Jessica had no wish to be taken under Caryn's wing like a homeless child. Dislike she understood; pity she could not stand.

"Wouldn't you rather have some company?" Caryn asked, her tone more subdued but no less friendly.

Ignoring Caryn's attempts at conversation, Jessica pulled out a pencil and started to draw.

"Well, then . . . I guess I'll leave you alone," Caryn said, voice muted. She moved to another table. Jessica continued drawing, ignoring Caryn and the teacher, who was droning on about locker assignments.

Mrs. Katherine asked Caryn to help distribute the locks, and when Caryn had finished, she lingered a moment at Jessica's table. Jessica wondered grimly at the girl's persistence.

"I've never been able to figure these out,"

Caryn muttered as she fiddled with her lock. She spun the combination a dozen times without success. "Maybe it's broken . . . You want to give it a try?"

Jessica plucked the lock from Caryn's hands and had it open in a second. "Hope you don't need to use the locker too much this year."

"How do these things work?" Caryn laughed at herself cheerfully.

"Figure it out yourself," Jessica answered as she shut the lock and tossed it back to Caryn.

"What did I do to you?" Caryn asked, finally deflated, and Jessica wouldn't have been surprised to see her eyes start to tear. "Why do you have to be so nasty to me?"

"It's who I am," Jessica snapped, closing her notebook and putting it away. "Learn to live with it."

She turned her back to Caryn as Mrs. Katherine led the class to their lockers. The girl didn't try to talk to Jessica again for the rest of the day. No one else did either; besides the arrival of Caryn, nothing had changed.

CHAPTER 2

"HOW WAS YOUR FIRST DAY of school?"
Caryn's mother asked as soon as the girl entered the kitchen.

Caryn's mother, Hasana Rashida, was a slightly plump, attractive woman with hair of a rich brown, cropped in a serious yet flattering style. She was obviously tired from her day at the bookstore, of which she was the new manager, so Caryn decided not to bother her with details of the icy putdowns she had received that morning.

"It wasn't awful," she answered instead as she fished a spoon from the silverware drawer and went to serve herself some ice cream.

The thought of Jessica made her uneasy. There was something in Jessica's aura that she hadn't been able to identify — something darker than normal. At first, it had almost kept Caryn from approaching. After only one day, she could see that it also kept other students away.

Of course, that was logical. Caryn wouldn't have been in this town if Jessica had been a normal high-school student.

Caryn had tried despite her unease to get to know Jessica, more because the girl had seemed so alone than because Caryn had been asked to do so.

Prompted by these thoughts, she asked, "Where's Dominique?"

Hasana sighed. "She left to deal with some trouble involving her daughters, but she should be back soon."

Dominique Vida was one of the few people who could give Caryn the chills just by entering the room. She was the leader of the oldest living line of witches, and her power was impressive. She was the one who had tracked down Jessica's address and maneuvered Caryn and Hasana into this town, finding a house for them and employment for Hasana in less than two weeks.

Either despite this power or because of it, the woman was emotionally cold as ice in almost any situation. She needed to be: Dominique Vida was a vampire hunter. She could not allow emotion to cause hesitation in a fight.

If anyone else had asked Caryn to move into this town, where she could barely breathe for the aura of vampires, she would have refused. But Dominique was the leader of all four lines of witches, including the Smoke line — Caryn's own.

Dominique could order Caryn to go into the vampires' lairs alone, and Caryn would do so or risk losing her title as a witch. As antisocial as Jessica seemed to be, at least watching the writer didn't seem dangerous.

Following the same train of thought as her daughter, Hasana asked, "Did you meet Jessica?"

"Yes. She hated me on sight," Caryn answered gloomily. "And considering how she's treated, I'm not surprised."

Caryn had been shocked at the way Jessica's classmates seemed to view her — as if she was a poisonous spider. One of them, an athletic senior who'd been flirting with Caryn only a few minutes before, had called

Jessica a witch. Hurt by his words, Caryn had needed to swallow an argument; Jessica was further from being a witch than the boy who had made the accusation.

Caryn glanced down at her bowl, her appetite gone. Her ice cream was melting.

CHAPTER 3

ANNE CONFRONTED JESSICA as soon as she walked in the front door. "You're late."

"Sorry," Jessica answered sardonically. "They love me so much, they asked me to stay a bit longer."

"Jessica . . . on the first day of school?" Anne's voice was heavy with disappointment.

"Learn the art of sarcasm," Jessica suggested. "I needed to walk off some energy, so I swung by the woods on my way home."

"Thank god." Anne smiled and started to fill out the forms that the school had mailed home. An awkward moment went by in silence.

"Anything interesting happen at school?"

Anne asked eventually, though Jessica could tell that her mind was not on the question.

"Nope," Jessica answered absently as she searched through her bag for a letter one of her teachers had given out for parents. She handed it to Anne.

After scanning the letter, Anne asked, "How are your teachers?"

"Fine."

"That's nice."

As usual, their conversation was more of a mandatory social gesture than a method of communication. Anne and Jessica had learned long before that they had nothing in common and had little chance of ever engaging in a truly two-sided talk about anything. Occasionally one actually paid attention to what the other was saying, but such circumstances usually led to arguments.

Another moment of silence ensued.

"I'm going to my room," Jessica announced finally. Leaving her backpack on the couch, she went upstairs and into the dimly lit cavern she had created for herself.

The windows were covered by heavy black curtains, and the shades were down. A small beam of light squeezed underneath the curtains, but that was all.

The bed, which was little more than a mattress on wheels, had been pushed into a corner. The sheets and comforter were black, as were all but one of the pillows. The exception was deep violet and made of fake suede. Anne had bought the pillow for Jessica several years ago, when she had still been attempting to influence the girl's tastes. Besides the pillow and Jessica's magenta Lava lamp, there was little else in the room that wasn't black.

A laptop computer and printer stood out brightly against their dark surroundings. They sat atop a black wooden desk, which they shared with a strewn assortment of floppy disks. The computer was one of the few things Jessica cherished. Here, in the shadowed niche she had created for herself, she churned out the novels that had been her escape from the world since she moved to Ramsa.

The twenty-nine manuscripts that she had written in the past five years, the brown envelopes that held her contracts for two of them, and a few copies of the published book *Tiger, Tiger* were the only other non-black objects in the room.

It had been only two years earlier that

she had first begun the search for a publisher; she could hardly believe how quickly things had gone since. Her first book, *Tiger, Tiger,* had been released about a week before, under the pen name Ash Night. The second one, *Dark Flame,* was presently sitting on her editor's desk awaiting the woman's comments.

Jessica flopped down onto her bed and looked up at the ceiling. Sometimes ideas for her books would strike as she lay like this, staring into oblivion, but usually they came from her dreams.

Even while she was writing, it was as if she was in a dream — one which her waking mind did not understand. She never quite knew what was happening in any of the numerous novels that she was working on at any given time. But she had learned not to read the manuscripts until they were finished. The only time she had broken that pattern, the flow of words had abruptly stopped. That had been the only story she disliked. The scenes written after she had read it seemed forced and unnatural. Trying to think them up had been a chore.

She didn't realize that she had drifted into

sleep until she was awakened by Anne's knock on her door.

"Jessica?"

"What?" she asked tiredly.

"It's dinnertime," Anne announced. "Are you going to come down?"

Jessica closed her eyes for a moment more and then got up and turned on her computer.

"I'm not hungry," she called to Anne. "Go ahead and eat without me."

"Jessica—"

"I'll eat later, Anne," she snapped. Normally she would have at least joined Anne for dinner, just to maintain the illusion of a familial relationship. But when she was in the mood to write, that pull was stronger than her desire to get along with her adopted mother.

CHAPTER 4

WITHIN FIVE MINUTES Jessica was writing quickly, lost in the bubble of her imagination. The entire night passed as she typed. It was sunrise when the flow of words halted.

Exhausted, Jessica turned off the computer, stood to stretch, and fell into bed and a sleep filled with nightmares.

Jazlyn collapsed to her knees, unable to stand any longer. Her head pounded as her body fought the strange blood that was trying to overtake her system.

She knew this sensation. She had felt it once

before, on the day she had died, years ago. It had not hurt so much then. It had not hurt to die.

It had not hurt to die . . .

Why did it hurt so much to live again?

Her vision went black as her heart beat for the first time in more than thirty years. She drew a slow, painful breath.

The heart in her chest labored, unaccustomed to its task. Her lungs burned with the constant intake of oxygen, which seemed to sear her throat. All the muscles of her torso cramped each time she inhaled.

Finally she fell into blissful unconsciousness.

Jessica woke, gasping for breath.

That same dream had frequented her sleep for years, but she had yet to become used to it. The pain was always so vivid.

She turned on the Lava lamp and let the glow of magenta light calm her. The clock read 6:13 A.M. Though it was less than an hour after she had fallen asleep, she was no longer tired. As always, that dream had forced fatigue far away.

After showering and dressing quickly, she paused to study herself in front of the full-length mirror in the bathroom. Jessica well knew she had a body and face to die for.

At five feet, five inches tall, she was slender but not bony and had well-toned muscles despite the fact that she rarely worked out. Her skin was naturally fair and had been kept that way by her aversion to sunlight. Unlike those of many girls her age, Jessica's complexion was flawless and always had been. Her long jet-black hair tumbled around a face with high cheekbones, full lips, and expressive green eyes.

Yet despite her attractive appearance, Jessica had never so much as had a date. Occasionally that fact bothered her, though she usually had plainer insults to deal with than oblique dismissals from the boys in her grade.

Annoyed, she finally turned away from her reflection. Again she'd been unable to find the flaw that made people hesitate when they saw her on the street or in the hall.

Downstairs in the kitchen, Anne was finishing a batch of pancakes.

"Morning, Jessica," Anne said as she slid two of the pancakes onto a plate. "Sit."

Jessica sat. She was in no hurry this morning, and the pancakes smelled delicious. She realized that she had eaten very little the day before.

"Smells good," she offered.

Anne smiled. "Thank you. I do try."

By the time she left for school, Jessica was in a good mood. She even had the heart to smile at Mrs. Katherine when she saw her in front of the building, and the teacher returned her gesture with a nod. Then Caryn walked by, and Jessica's cheer vanished.

CHAPTER 5

As she entered the building, Jessica came upon a group of girls who had gathered near the main office.

"Nice body," she heard one of them whisper, referring to someone in the office.

"Who is he?" another girl asked.

"No idea," the first one answered. "But you've got to admit he's cute."

"Cute?" a third girl repeated. "He is totally *hot*."

Jessica couldn't see the subject of this profound conversation. *Probably some handsome blond substitute who will turn out to be the most hated teacher in the school,* she thought pessimistically.

"Who are you looking at?" she asked the three gawking girls.

The quietest, a senior named Kathy, looked over her shoulder, recognized Jessica, grabbed her friends' arms, and pulled the girls away.

Jessica scowled as she watched them go. At least most people were *subtle* about moving away from her.

She quickly forgot the girls' behavior, however, when she glanced into the office and saw the object of their admiration.

His face could have been modeled after the portrait on a Roman coin. Hair the color of raven feathers contrasted with his fair skin, and when he turned a bit she saw that a few strands had fallen across his eyes, shading them. He was dressed entirely in black, except for a gold chain around his neck. The pendant on the chain looked like a cross, but Jessica couldn't be sure from where she was standing.

A shock of recognition struck her. *Aubrey.*

Aubrey was, without a doubt, her favorite character from the books she had written. He had been the villain in *Tiger, Tiger* and the main character in *Dark Flame*. Gorgeous, powerful, and somewhat mysterious, he was every teenage girl's fantasy . . . or at least, he was hers. Considering her present status in the world of teenagers, she couldn't pretend to speak for the rest of the female population.

Of course, Aubrey was a vampire.

Get a grip, Jessica. You write fiction, she reminded herself. *Aubrey doesn't exist.* She would hardly have minded if her vampire hero *had* existed, but such a thing was impossible. Vampires were not real.

Yet the resemblance between this new boy and Aubrey was uncanny, and the sense of familiarity lingered despite her efforts to shake it. She forced herself to turn away and walk to her homeroom before the boy could notice her watching him.

She sat in the back of the room once again, and this time no one came to talk to her. Caryn looked over once from the group she seemed to have been accepted into, but Jessica sent a fierce gaze her way and Caryn cringed, visibly shaken.

A few moments after attendance had been taken, the boy from the office walked in. He handed a form to Mrs. Katherine but didn't bother to explain why he was late.

"Alex Remington?" Mrs. Katherine asked, reading the form.

He nodded, barely paying attention to the teacher as he sought out an empty seat.

Alex paused when he saw Caryn, who was watching him with wide eyes. Unlike most of the other females in the room, Caryn looked terrified.

When the bell rang, Jessica watched with curiosity as Caryn pulled on her backpack and slipped quickly through the crowd and out of the room. She was clearly being careful to stay as far from Alex Remington as she could.

Before Alex had even reached the door, a girl named Shannon caught up with him. Jessica could recognize Shannon's methods of flirtation a mile away and shook her head in disgust. Shannon already had a boyfriend, but that had never stopped her when there was a drop-dead-gorgeous male in her line of vision.

Jessica was about to leave when Alex glanced up for a moment, meeting her gaze over Shannon's shoulder. His eyes were jet-black and shadowed by dark lashes. Jessica smiled wryly in response to the amusement she saw in those eyes—no doubt a reaction to Shannon's not-so-subtle advances.

Then something Shannon said caught his attention and he looked away from Jessica, returning his gaze to his more assertive admirer.

A bit reluctantly, Jessica headed down the hall, leaving Alex at the mercy of Shannon the Conquerer.

CHAPTER 6

JESSICA WANDERED into the courtyard at lunchtime, having no desire to sit alone at a table in the cafeteria so that she could be assaulted by the stench of the day's mystery meat.

Her thoughts traveled for a moment to Alex; she remembered how he had caught her eye. Then she mentally chided herself for focusing on a guy who probably had already forgotten she existed. And even if he hadn't, he would never be desperate enough to risk his social standing by associating with the leper of Ramsa High.

She pulled an unlined notebook and a mechanical pencil from her backpack and proceeded to sketch, simply for something to do with her hands, as she discreetly watched the people around her.

Shannon was standing with a few of her friends, but instead of talking to them, she was staring intensely across the courtyard at Alex. Alex, leaning casually against a tree, was smirking slightly as another boy berated him. Jessica recognized the guy as Shannon's boyfriend, and she judged by his posture and tone of voice that he had heard about Shannon's conversation with Alex that morning.

Finally Alex seemed to lose his patience. He locked eyes with the other boy, who, though a few inches taller than Alex and much broader, took a step back. The boy said something Jessica couldn't hear and left quickly.

Jessica shook her head, not surprised. Something about Alex made it evident he wasn't someone to mess with.

As Jessica had watched the confrontation, she had continued to draw. Now she looked down at the pencil sketch and felt a chill run through her.

Even though her model had been nearby, the likeness was remarkable. But the thing that struck her the most was the pendant, which she hadn't yet been able to look at closely but had somehow drawn in careful detail.

The cross was upside down and carefully molded with a viper twined around it. It was the same design as the one that Aubrey wore, and it startled Jessica to see that she had drawn it into her portrait of Alex.

"Mind if I join you?" someone asked.

Not just someone. *Alex.* Jessica recognized his voice and whipped her notebook shut. His tone was confident, unmarred by adolescent awkwardness. Hearing his silk-smooth voice made her shiver, because she was once again assaulted by a wave of familiarity.

Snap out of it, Jessica ordered herself. Over her mental argument, she heard her voice calmly reply to Alex, "Go ahead."

Suspicious of his motives, she couldn't immediately come up with anything more to say. The last time any guy had tried to talk to her, he had done so only on a dare. With that painful memory in mind, she kept her expression cool, waiting for Alex Remington to explain himself.

As he sat down near her, she studied his

appearance. The pendant was exactly as she had drawn it — exactly like Aubrey's.

"Do you always keep to yourself out here?" he asked.

"Do you always go out of your way to talk to people who look like they want to be alone?" she answered, instinctively defensive. She bit her tongue after speaking the words. If Alex actually wanted to get to know her, she was an idiot to try to chase him off.

He just looked amused. "Would you prefer to be alone, or are you avoiding someone in particular?" As he asked this, he glanced over at the windows of the cafeteria. Jessica followed his gaze and noticed Caryn sitting inside with a group of other seniors.

"If I was trying to avoid anyone, it would be Caryn," she answered truthfully. "She seems convinced that my inner child needs a friend."

A mixture of empathy and annoyance crossed Alex's features. Jessica felt confident that the annoyance was reserved for Caryn.

"It's her nature to try to draw people out of the dark," he said.

"You two know each other?"

"Unfortunately," he answered. The scorn in his voice was palpable.

He silently watched Caryn for a moment, until she looked up as if she could feel his gaze. When she saw Jessica and Alex sitting together, she stood, gathered her belongings, and hurried away.

"She sure doesn't try to draw *you* out of the dark," Jessica commented.

"They've tried, and they've failed miserably," was his reply.

CHAPTER 7

CARYN HAD RETREATED to the school library after seeing Jessica with the creature who was calling himself Alex. She had a study hall there soon, anyway; other students were already spilling out of the cafeteria and going to their classes.

She had been staring out the window for about five minutes when she suddenly saw Alex and Jessica walk past. It seemed there was no escape from them.

"Are you stalking me?" she heard Jessica say to Alex in a light, maybe even flirtatious, tone. Caryn frowned at how easily Jessica seemed to trust him. Alex was the last creature on Earth that any human should trust.

"Why would I do that?" Alex asked with pretend innocence.

Why indeed? Caryn thought. *Maybe because you're a manipulative leech?* If only Jessica knew what she was talking to.

"Anyway, I'm not quite so obvious when I'm stalking someone," Alex was saying to Jessica, amusement in his voice.

Caryn shook her head. *Of course you are,* she thought. *If they don't know you're there, they aren't afraid.*

Suddenly she heard his mocking voice clearly in her mind. *I suppose you would know from experience?*

She threw up her mental shields, even though she knew they were little better than glass against his kind. *Get out of my head,* she thought angrily. Alex laughed in return.

Meanwhile, he and Jessica had continued to speak. It was obvious that Jessica had no knowledge of the silent conversation that had been going on. Her tone was jovial and unguarded, as if she was speaking to a friend.

Friends with the leeches but not with the humans, Caryn thought bitterly.

She couldn't exactly blame Jessica, though. Even knowing the truth about Alex, Caryn herself could barely sense his bubble of mental control. Without conscious effort he kept humans in thrall, so that they were comfortable around him despite their instinct to avoid his kind.

Only twice during the day had Caryn seen him let down his guard: with Shannon that morning and with the boy who had insulted him at lunch. Shannon had quickly stopped her flirtation and slunk away but had managed to laugh about her sudden unease when describing the situation to Caryn later.

Caryn forced herself to start her homework rather than think about Alex and Jessica any longer. She had no fighting skills with which to defend Jessica physically. And the girl had made it clear that she wanted no part of Caryn's friendship, so she certainly wouldn't be willing to heed her warning.

Caryn was not going to get in Alex's way — especially here, surrounded by so many defenseless humans. Arguing with a vampire in the middle of a crowd would only get people killed.

CHAPTER 8

AFTER SCHOOL Jessica took the bus to the center of town. She walked to the bookstore, hoping to find *Tiger, Tiger* on the shelves. The book was supposed to have come out more than a week before, but this was the first chance Jessica had had to look for it. The advance copies she had at home didn't hold quite the same allure as the sight of her work in a bookstore display.

Jessica sighed when she saw Caryn browsing the shelves, but she wasn't about to let the annoying teen chase her away.

"Oh . . . hi, Jessica," Caryn said, sounding surprised. "You looking for anything?"

"A book. What else would I be in a bookstore for?" Jessica answered crossly.

It took her only a second to spot *Tiger, Tiger* on the shelf next to Caryn, and she reached past the girl to grab a copy. As the book was written under Jessica's pseudonym, Ash Night, Caryn wouldn't be able to connect Jessica with it. Even so, Caryn's eyes widened when she saw the book.

"I've read that one," she said in a voice that sounded falsely casual.

"So have I," Jessica answered, turning away from Caryn and toward the counter.

"I wonder what the author is like," Caryn commented. "Where do you suppose her ideas come from?"

Jessica ignored Caryn effortlessly until she added, "What if it was all real? If Ash Night's vampires actually existed? If Ather and Risika and Aubrey—"

Jessica spun on Caryn as she spoke that last name. "Vampires don't exist," she snapped. "Get over it." After having had this conversation with herself all day long, she was glad to finally have an excuse to say the words aloud.

"But—"

"Caryn, I've been subtle, rude, and even

offensive," Jessica interrupted. "Now it's time for direct." She met Caryn's delicate blue eyes with a glacier-cold glare. "I don't care if you think vampires exist. I don't want to talk about it, just like I don't want to chat about combination locks or anything else. I don't want to talk to you at all. Do you understand?"

With a bit of a sigh, Caryn nodded, deflated.

That had been rather satisfying. Next Jessica just had to convince herself that Alex Remington wasn't the Antichrist, and she could return to the regularly scheduled tedium of her daily life.

"Cold," she heard behind her. "Very cold. I approve completely."

Jessica turned and saw Alex leaning against a shelf. His gaze as he watched Caryn hurry away reminded Jessica of a wolf watching a rabbit run to cover.

"Maybe I'm paranoid, but I could swear you've been following me." The words were out of Jessica's mouth before she had a chance to consider them. Hearing her own tone, she almost choked. If she caught herself flirting, she was likely to become ill.

"On and off," he answered vaguely, and

didn't add anything more. He turned to wander down the aisle, glancing from shelf to shelf as if looking for something. After a few yards he looked over his left shoulder to see if she was still behind him, and it occurred to her that *she* was following *him*. Embarrassed, she stopped doing so.

"Anything good in here?" he asked, returning to the shelf where Jessica had found *Tiger, Tiger*.

"What's your definition of good?" she asked, making a point not to move toward him.

He pulled a book from the shelf: *Renegade*, by Elizabeth Charcoal. Showing it to Jessica, he said, "You'll love it. Trust me."

"You've read this?" Jessica had seen a magazine article about the author, though she hadn't had a chance to read the book. Elizabeth Charcoal claimed that she was a vampire, and that *Renegade* was actually her autobiography.

"I know the author," Alex answered matter-of-factly. "She gave me an autographed copy of the manuscript. Right after she tried to slit my throat, but why sweat the details?"

"Oh, really?" Jessica said skeptically.

He was either teasing her or trying to impress her.

He shrugged. "We got into an argument."

"Does this happen to you often?"

"Fairly frequently," he answered, his tone nonchalant. "Elizabeth and I don't like each other very much, but her book is . . . interesting. It's the kind of thing you'd like."

"How do *you* know what I like to read?"

"I can tell," he answered cryptically, and then he turned to the checkout. He paused so that she could catch up and walk beside him, not behind.

The woman at the counter looked at Alex with contempt and whispered something under her breath.

"Hasana, what a surprise." Alex greeted her coolly. He smiled malevolently. The woman glared at him, but he ignored it.

"You two know each other?" Jessica asked foolishly, seeing the angry sparks fly between them.

"Hasana is Caryn's mother," Alex offered, as if that explained everything. Jessica remembered Caryn's reaction that morning when she had first seen Alex, and wondered what had happened between him and this family.

"Watch out for this guy," Hasana warned, nodding toward Alex. "He probably knows more about you than your taste in books."

"And how could that be?" Jessica asked dryly.

"I can read your mind, and learn your secret fears and darkest desires," Alex answered.

Jessica paused, examining his expression. She had written those exact words, Aubrey's words, in *Dark Flame*, the novel that was presently waiting on her editor's desk. She couldn't remember whether she had used them in *Tiger, Tiger.*

"Do you always talk like that?" she asked, unnerved.

He looked at her challengingly as he said, "Don't you know?"

She just shook her head, alarmed but unwilling to show it.

As Alex paid for his book, Jessica realized that she was still holding *Tiger, Tiger.* She placed it on the counter, not intending to buy it; she had plenty of copies at home.

Alex's gaze drifted to the cover, and his expression leapt immediately from amusement to anger. He spun away and, without another word, stalked out of the store. Jessica was left staring after him, too shocked to react.

"If I were you, I'd just avoid him," Hasana advised.

"Why? Is he going to hurt me?" Jessica's sarcasm was sharpened by her confusion regarding Alex.

"Unless you keep away from him, he most likely will," Hasana answered seriously. "He has a temper."

Jessica was out of sharp remarks. To hide her discomfort, she picked up the copy of *Tiger, Tiger* and said, "I guess I'll put this away before it makes anyone else freak out."

"If you want it, just keep it," Hasana answered softly. "You *are* the author."

Jessica froze, dumbfounded.

"I'm sorry," Hasana said quickly. "I just—"

"How did you know?" Jessica interrupted, annoyed to learn that this woman had connected her to Ash Night. She had used a pen name to *avoid* recognition.

"I've read it, and I . . . recognized you as the author," Hasana fumbled. "You just have a look about you . . ."

"What *look*?"

"Never mind," Hasana said, shaking her head. "Take the book and the advice, and ignore me."

She turned away, suddenly very busy with some papers, and Jessica left in a daze.

CHAPTER 9

AUBREY HAD LEFT THE STORE to avoid hurting someone — probably the witch.

Though he had a house on the fringe of town, he preferred to spend his time in the heart of New Mayhem, in his room behind the nightclub known as Las Noches. There he paced angrily, wondering what to do about the human called Jessica.

She didn't know that everything she wrote was true. She thought vampires were just another myth. She thought her characters were just figments of her own imagination. She had no idea what Alex was.

That wasn't quite true. He knew that Jessica had recognized him the instant she saw him. Only her human rationality had kept her from believing that Alex Remington was actually Aubrey.

Aubrey had heard of the author Ash Night through a young vampire who worked as an editor at Night's publishing company. The vampire had even given Aubrey a copy of the *Dark Flame* manuscript. The news of this book had quickly spread through the vampiric community, as it had when Elizabeth Charcoal had published her autobiography.

The difference was that Ash Night was not writing about herself, but about things she had no right to know. *Dark Flame* was Aubrey's own history, which no one but he knew in total. Yet Ash Night had written his past correctly, down to the last detail.

Aubrey didn't mind the thought of *Dark Flame*'s being published. In his history he had almost always been stronger than those around him. However, the others who were mentioned in the manuscript came across as often weak, and in the vampiric world, there was no worse threat to one's position than an apparent weakness. *Dark Flame* had earned its author some dangerous enemies.

The vampire from the publishing company had not worked with Ash Night di-

rectly, and she must not have known about
the author's first book. Seeing *Tiger, Tiger*
in the store today had taken Aubrey
completely by surprise. The cover made it
strikingly clear whom the book was about.
Despite the artist's ignorance of his subject, Aubrey had instantly recognized the
portrayal of Risika. He had lived this book
as well—or unlived it, as the case might
be. He knew what would be printed on its
pages.

Aubrey lightly touched the scar that
stretched across his left shoulder, which
Risika had given to him a few years ago. For
the first time in nearly three thousand years
he had lost a fight, and he had lost it badly.
Risika could have killed him in the end. Instead, she had taken his blood and let him
live. The action had opened his mind to her
completely; she could now read him as easily
as he could read most humans.

The sight of the book was like the thrust
of a knife into his still-bleeding pride.

Aubrey had been the first of his kind to
search out the author, and most of the other
vampires were satisfied by the knowledge
that he was dealing with the problem.

Though Jessica had requested that her

true name and address remain private, Aubrey had easily pulled the information from the mind of her editor. Her town, Ramsa, New York, was only a stone's throw away from his home in New Mayhem, one of the strongest vampiric cities in the United States. Aubrey had drifted into Ramsa to see how much of a threat this Ash Night was.

What had he expected? Anything but what he found: a seventeen-year-old human who had no apparent connection to the vampire world. She did, however, have a darkness in her aura that was almost vampiric. This close to New Mayhem, Jessica's aura was strengthened by the vampires in the area. Humans reacted to it instinctively and drew away from her, as they had from Aubrey until he had started influencing their minds.

He had tried to influence Jessica. He should have been able to reach into her mind and tell her to stop writing. With any other human the task would have been easy, but with Jessica he had been blocked completely. That fact alone had fascinated him enough to refrain from killing her the first time he'd been given the chance.

Indeed, there were many things about

Jessica that interested him despite his usual distaste for humans. Foremost was her unnerving lack of reaction when he had caught her eye earlier. Most humans would have become disoriented, momentarily trapped in his gaze, but Jessica had been unaffected.

Aubrey closed his eyes for a moment, taking a breath to calm himself. He stopped pacing and once again wore the dispassionate mask that he had developed over his many years of life.

But the craving for movement would not die as cleanly as he had hoped, so he left his room and walked down the short hallway to Las Noches.

The nightclub's atmosphere was intense. Red strobe lights flashed through the room, disorienting everyone but those who had spent as much time inside the place as Aubrey had. Bass-heavy music pounded from speakers hidden somewhere in the shadowed ceiling, and mirrors covered the four walls. Risika had shattered every inch of these mirrors during her fight with Aubrey, so the numerous reflections were now distorted.

Until Jessica saw Las Noches, walked inside, and tried to keep her mind from spinning, she would never be able to accurately imagine the psychedelic bar and nightclub that was the dark heart of New Mayhem.

Of course, Jessica didn't believe that New Mayhem even existed.

Now, in the hour before sunset, the crowd was the usual mix of humans and vampires. The mortals were comforted by the sunlight that still bathed the world outside; most of the vampires in the room would not hunt until after dark. The bartender on duty was an ebony-eyed girl named Kaei. With her pale skin and the curtain of ink-black hair that fell down her back, Kaei had looked like the traditional vampire even when she'd been human. She had been born in Mayhem and had been responsible for its nearly complete destruction three hundred years earlier. She had offered Aubrey her blood more than once, and in return he had probably saved her life a dozen times.

"Moira was looking for you," Kaei told Aubrey as he approached. "She mentioned something about helping you 'dice the writer into bite-sized pieces.'" Moira had complained many times recently that Ash Night had made her seem weak. The author had not needed to try very hard. Though Moira was strong in comparison to most others of their kind, she was one of the weakest of their line. She had been changed more than five hundred years before Aubrey but had never gained his strength.

Most of their line had been strong as humans; that was how they attracted the attention of the vampires who would ultimately change them. Fala had met and fallen in love with Moira, then changed the human woman to save her life.

Despite Moira's weakness, she and her blood sister Fala were feared because of their reputation for being fond of causing pain. Moira had been born before the Aztecs, and shortly after she'd been changed, she had pulled the heart out of one of their priests with her bare hands.

"Fala asked for you too," Kaei continued, her expression grim. "She was talking about turning the author into ash — making her 'fit her name better.'" Unlike Moira, who preferred weaponry, Fala was fond of fire.

Aubrey sighed, having no desire to deal with either of the two vampires. "Maybe they could draw straws," he answered wearily.

"Do what you will," Kaei answered, knowing that what she said rarely mattered. She walked away without another word.

Aubrey pulled one of the unlabeled bottles from under the bar. Though not exactly sure what it was, he knew it wouldn't harm him. He could down a liter of cyanide and not notice any effect. Some of these bottles held wine, others liquor, and others blood that was always cold. How the bar was kept stocked was a mystery, as there was rarely a bartender working and the drinks were all free.

CHAPTER 10

AUBREY WAS STILL AT THE BAR when he heard a familiar voice behind him.

"Welcome back," Jager said in his usual cool tone. Jager was the second oldest in their line and one of the few vampires who might rival Aubrey for pure strength. However, he was rarely interested in fighting.

"Did you meet Night?" Jager asked when Aubrey did not instantly volunteer the information.

"I did," Aubrey answered, not elaborating.

"Did you kill him?" It was an offhand question. Killing was the logical way to deal with a human who could be a threat to their kind. Whether or not she knew it, Jessica possessed truths that were dangerous to the vampire world—and she had chosen to share them.

"Her," Aubrey corrected. "No, I didn't kill her."

He didn't know quite why he hadn't killed Jessica. It would not have been difficult, and the death would not have created much of a stir, after a few whispered words into the minds of Anne Allodola and Ash Night's business associates.

"I hope Risika isn't a bad loser when it comes to bets," Jager commented. "She assumed you'd kill the author."

"She would," Aubrey answered dryly. *What would Jessica think,* he wondered, *if she knew there were bets being made about her potential death?*

"May I ask why you *didn't* kill her?" Jager said, not disguising his curiosity.

Aubrey wondered about the answer himself. The phrase "she's beautiful" came to mind, and of course it was true. Jessica seemed almost to embody the graceful perfection of a vampire. But Aubrey had never before hesitated to kill someone because she was attractive.

More than her physical appearance, Jessica had a rare aura of strength about her. Aubrey remembered Ash Night's describing him as having the same kind of aura while he had been human, but he had seen it in very few others. Risika had been one of the exceptions; that strength had drawn Aubrey to her before she had ever caught Ather's eye. Now Jessica was another.

"Is the question too difficult?" Jager asked, his tone patronizing.

Aubrey resorted to the simplest answer. "I wasn't in the mood."

Jager accepted the explanation, and the two vampires sat awhile in companionable silence.

Suddenly the fiery Fala appeared in front of them.

"I see you've returned from your little game in the sunlight," she purred at Aubrey. Her voice was like poisoned chocolate, deceptively smooth and sweet. As she brushed by Jager, she gave him a quick kiss on the cheek.

Fala was Jager's first fledgling. Born in Egypt, she had naturally dark skin that had paled little in the almost five thousand years she'd been a vampire. Her black hair was pulled back from her face by bloodred combs, but that was the only bit of color in her otherwise black outfit.

"I suppose you've met Night," Fala spat, as if the name was not one to be mentioned in polite society. "Is she quite dead, I hope? Even better, is she writhing in pain somewhere?"

"She's alive," Aubrey answered, not in the mood to exchange sadistic banter with Fala.

"Mind if I kill her for you?" Fala asked casually as she walked behind the bar and poured herself a drink from Aubrey's bottle. "This is good," she commented, holding the bottle up to the red light, which did not help to illuminate its contents. "Anyone know what it is?"

She emptied the rest of the liquid into her glass, then threw the unlabeled bottle over her shoulder. The bottle shattered, and several people at the tables turned at the sound. One human stood up and brushed glass off her jeans, but she didn't seem upset. Breaking glass was hardly an unusual occurrence at Las Noches.

Fala sighed luxuriously as she turned back to Aubrey and Jager. "I love the sound of breaking glass. Now, about Ash—"

"No, you can't kill her for me," Aubrey interrupted.

"You're going to stop me?" she asked, her voice going lower, slightly menacing.

"I have more of a quarrel with her than you do," he answered coldly, not bothering to explain the statement.

"Unless she has drawn blood, Aubrey, you have *nothing*," Fala snapped back, stalking closer to him.

Fala was referring to one of the few standing rules of their kind: blood claim. Humans, unless they lived in New Mayhem, were free prey of any vampire. However, if a human drew the blood of a vampire, that human could only be hunted by the vampire who had been harmed. Had Jessica attacked Aubrey and somehow made him bleed, Fala would have been unable to hurt Jessica without Aubrey's permission.

"She hasn't, and she never will," he answered.

"You wouldn't admit to being wounded by a human even if you had been," Fala scoffed. She finished her drink and threw the glass over her shoulder. "But I suppose you wouldn't be in such a good mood if you'd lost *another* fight."

She said nothing more. Aubrey struck her with his mind, and she fell backward into the bar, hissing in anger. Several heads turned toward them, and a few humans chose that time to exit Las Noches; it was dangerous to be in the same room with two fighting vampires.

Jager was still nearby, and he was watching the argument with narrowed eyes.

"Would you care to repeat that?" Aubrey asked Fala, his voice cold as ice as he casually threw another bolt of power at her, causing her to double over in pain. He hadn't even broken a sweat.

"Aubrey." Jager spoke only his name, a calm but clear warning.

Aubrey answered by drawing back his power instead of hitting Fala again. Jager would not start a fight over what had happened thus far; Fala wouldn't appreciate the help. But even so, Aubrey knew that Jager was too fond of Fala to look the other way if she was truly threatened.

"Damn you, Aubrey," Fala cursed. She scowled but was wise enough not to insult him again.

"Already been done," he answered calmly.

"Damn you again!" she shouted, delivering a glare that would have stilled serpents in their dens.

"Too late," he quipped. "And after five

thousand years, I'd think you could come up with something better than that."

Fala growled but didn't attempt to attack him. Though she was far older than he was, he had always been stronger, and he was a better fighter. If she fought back, she would lose.

"Fine," she snarled. "But if you don't kill the human, or otherwise dispose of her, I *will*. Is that perfectly understandable to you, Aubrey?"

"Yes."

In the next moment they were both gone, Aubrey retreating to his room. The nightclub's heavy music reverberated through the building, but he was used to it. He fell into bed and a sleep of complete oblivion. Like most of his kind, he did not dream.

CHAPTER 11

WHEN AUBREY WOKE he brought himself to the edge of Red Rock, the forest that surrounded New Mayhem and fringed Ramsa. The ability to instantly move from one place to another was a power he used often, as he had for more than two thousand years.

The full moon was about a week away still, but Aubrey could easily sense a few untrained witches and some werewolves lurking in the busy forest. There were also several vampires nearby, all of Mira's bloodline.

Ramsa was supposedly Mira's territory, but that barely worried Aubrey. Mira, though ancient, was one of the weakest of their kind, and her fledglings were little stronger than most humans. Few in Mira's bloodline had lived through Fala's extermination of them a few hundred years before, and now they were hardly even considered part of the vampiric community. Most of them were so sensitive toward their prey that they only fed on animals and willing humans.

There was a party going on at a house on the edge of the woods. Shannon had unwittingly invited Aubrey to it, before he had frightened her. The house was filled with people, and the faint scent of alcohol floated from it to where Aubrey stood watching, many yards away. He easily reached out with his mind and sifted through the thoughts of those inside.

The minds he touched were hardly entertaining — either hazy from drinking, silly from joking, or angry from gossiping. He found Shannon quickly. She had drunk some beer and her defenses were down; little effort was necessary to convince her to come outside alone.

Shannon wandered absently into the woods, and jumped in surprise when she came upon Aubrey.

"Um . . . Hi, Alex."

She greeted him tentatively, glancing back at the house in obvious confusion as to how she had arrived here. Before she could decide to leave, he reached into her mind and her nervousness faded.

"Shannon, right?" he asked, taking a step toward her.

"Yeah," she answered with a coy smile. "Why are you hiding here in the —"

Sleep. Aubrey sent the command to her mind as soon as he was close enough to catch her as she fell.

She collapsed, unconscious in an instant, and he caught her without effort. He could have caught someone ten times her weight with no difficulty. Though he could control any human physically, he didn't relish the possibility that the girl would scream and attract inconvenient attention. It was easier to have her asleep as he fed. He had done this many times before.

He tilted Shannon's head back to expose the artery, which was covered by nothing more than a thin layer of skin. His canines, which looked normal enough most of the time, extended to razor-sharp points. These fangs pierced the skin of her throat quickly and precisely, and within moments he was lost in the sensation of the rich human blood that ran over his tongue and quenched his thirst.

CHAPTER 12

CARYN HAD SENSED Aubrey's presence even before she saw Shannon leave the party with a dazed look on her face. She had felt the pressure of his mind on Shannon's.

Caryn had no idea what she would do once she encountered Aubrey, but she felt compelled to follow Shannon anyway. A group of boys had bunched together at the door, and Caryn was delayed for a few minutes as she tried to slip through the throng. Once she was finally outside, it took her only a short moment to find the vampire and his prey. She could easily sense Aubrey's aura, which was like a shadow flickering just outside the normal spectrum of vision. She could feel his power slither across her skin.

This ability was her line's gift — or curse, as some would say. Though her family, the Smoke line, had always been healers, most witches were vampire hunters. Caryn had a witch's blood, which was sweeter and stronger than a human's, and a witch's knowledge, which made her dangerous to the vampires. But she did not have the ability to fight. She had always known herself to be easy prey, and had tried out of self-protection to avoid their kind, unless doing so meant risking an innocent person's life.

Throughout her childhood, Caryn had been taught to respect life, and to protect it whatever the cost. She knew Aubrey too well to look the other way while he cast his lure.

"Aubrey!" she called as soon as she had found him.

The vampire was standing several yards into the woods, holding Shannon, who was motionless. Aubrey had an arm around her waist to keep her from falling, and his other hand cradled the back of her neck. His lips were at her throat. Shannon was pale but still breathing.

"Aubrey!" Caryn shouted again when he didn't respond.

Aubrey glanced up and glared at her as he continued to feed. *What do you want?* he growled.

Caryn jumped at the intrusion into her mind but somehow managed to find her voice. "Let her go, Aubrey."

"Is that a threat?" Scorn laced his voice as he dropped Shannon. He mockingly licked a trace of blood from his lips.

Caryn hurried to Shannon's side. She was unconscious but would live.

"How many people have you murdered like this?" Caryn demanded, her voice wavering.

"I don't think you really want to know," Aubrey answered coolly.

"Don't you have any conscience at all?"

"Not that I know of," he said with nonchalance. "Now, much as I love your company, I really do prefer to dine alone."

He was enjoying this, Caryn realized. He could easily have avoided the argument by disappearing and finding prey elsewhere, but instead he was playing with her.

"You'll kill her," Caryn protested.

"So?" Aubrey responded, sounding

amused, as he took a step toward her. Caryn flinched but did not move away from Shannon. If he was determined to kill tonight, she had no hope of preventing it, but her conscience would not allow her to leave.

"Are you planning to stop me?" he mocked. "If you were one of your cousins, I might at least *pretend* to be worried . . . though probably not. As it is, I know you'd never fight me even if you had the strength."

He was speaking the truth. No one in her line had harmed another creature since Evelyn Smoke, the first of the Smoke line, had stopped hunting vampires.

"Please, Aubrey," Caryn entreated, beginning to despair.

"Caryn, go away. You're beginning to bore me."

"Let her go," Caryn persisted, though her tone was hardly commanding. She was sickened by his game, and worse, she worried what would happen when he reached the end of his patience.

"That would accomplish very little," Aubrey pointed out. "I would just have to draw someone else from the house. Would you like to say that this girl's life is more important than, oh, her boyfriend's? Or—"

"You're having a great time, aren't you?" Caryn finally shouted, standing and stalking toward him as her anger gave her courage.

Waiting for her to continue, Aubrey lounged casually against an oak tree. Had she been from any other line—Vida, or Arun, or even Light—she would have killed him then. But the last of the Light line had died nearly three hundred years earlier, and the Vidas and Aruns had other vampires to deal with that night. So Caryn Smoke did the only thing that her training would allow her to do in this situation.

She took a deep, calming breath and stretched out her left arm with the palm up, exposing the pale tracery of veins at her wrist.

"Here," she said softly, her fear almost hidden. "My blood is stronger than human blood." Her voice quaked for a moment, but she forced herself to continue. "You wouldn't need to kill me."

Aubrey's gaze flickered to the pulse point on her wrist, but that was the only sign that he cared for the offer at all. "And what is to stop me from draining you dry?"

"Your word that you won't."

She saw the amusement in his gaze. Had the situation been reversed, she would have understood the humor. Taking his word for her safety was like a vampire's accepting the word of any other witch. Most witches lied and broke promises almost by habit when it came to Aubrey's kind. Vampires weren't considered people, so even the proud Vida line had no hesitation about deceiving them. In general, only the Smoke line considered honesty important when dealing with Aubrey's kind.

A vampire's word was said to be broken as easily as a wineglass, and Caryn had no doubt that Aubrey's was just as fragile. In reality, the only thing that might keep her alive was Aubrey's awareness that killing a Smoke witch brought down instant retaliation from all the vampire hunters in the other lines.

Caryn's heartbeat quickened with fright, but she used all the discipline she'd been taught to keep her resolution from wavering.

Aubrey took the wrist she offered and used it to draw her toward him. He put a hand on her forehead and gently tilted her head back. Her heart rate tripled in an instant, but she balled her hands into fists to keep from trying to pull away.

Don't worry, she heard him say in her mind. *It won't hurt.*

She felt a sharp stinging when his teeth pierced her skin, but it faded almost immediately. The combined anesthesia of vampiric saliva and his whispering voice in her head dulled the pain completely. Caryn's legs gave out under the pressure of Aubrey's mind, and she felt him put an arm around her back to hold her up.

You taste good, he said absently.

I don't know whether to take that as a compliment or a threat, she mused. Her fear had disappeared, and her thoughts were becoming incoherent as she lost blood and his mind tightened its grip on her own.

Caryn tried to focus. She had been taught so much discipline . . . why couldn't she *think*?

She had been prepared for pain, but there was none. She felt extremely relaxed, as if she was floating . . . She was dreaming . . . wasn't she? Did it matter?

She imagined herself resting on a beach in the warm sun, or maybe meditating atop a mountain beneath the full moon. She was relaxed, peaceful, calm, happy to forget . . .

Forget what?

Caryn tried to focus, but it was nearly impossible. Aubrey's mind pulled at hers, numbing and soothing it. With intense effort, she drew herself out of her trance. There was far too much danger to forget what was happening.

His mind still held hers, and it was increasingly difficult not to let herself fall back into the seductive void. But if she gave in, would she ever surface again? He would probably kill her.

Would you rather it hurt?

Caryn had the vague idea that Aubrey was taunting her, but she could do nothing about it.

Eventually, after what seemed to be hours, Aubrey reluctantly pulled away. Caryn collapsed, suddenly aware again of her own body.

She was dizzy and weak, and her pulse was hurried as her heart attempted to circulate her thinned blood. Through foggy vision, she saw Aubrey hesitate, as if debating whether he really wanted to let her go.

Then he disappeared.

She put her head down for a moment, trying to clear her mind, then carefully crossed the clearing to make sure Shannon was all right. Hopefully, when the girl woke she would just assume she had drunk too much. She would never know how close she'd come to dying.

With this thought, Caryn put a hand over her own heart, feeling the rapid beating. Unlike Shannon, she was completely aware of how close Death had brushed by her tonight.

CHAPTER 13

JESSICA HAD BEEN WRITING all evening, but by the time midnight came the inspiration had died. She was restless and knew she wouldn't be able to fall asleep anytime soon. The best way she could think to burn some energy was to go for a walk.

The round moon lit her path through Red Rock Forest, and she soon found herself at her favorite spot: a large oak tree about a quarter of a mile in. She pulled herself onto one of its large branches and relaxed. Something about the night always calmed her.

Finally, under a broad canopy of leaves, she drifted into sleep.

Jazlyn's heart labored hard, unused to its task. Her lungs burned with the constant effort of breathing. But finally she fell into blissful unconsciousness.

Instead of the death-sleep that she had grown accustomed to, she dreamed of the world she was now trying to escape. She dreamed that she was running through a city street at midnight, chasing her frightened prey. She dreamed that she was flying far above the nighttime desert in the form of an eagle. She dreamed that she was walking in a graveyard, toward the grave of her once-husband.

Jazlyn woke gasping for breath. It took her several moments to realize where she was, which was something that hadn't happened to her in a long time. Her very survival had frequently depended on her ability to wake instantly.

During those confused moments, a vague memory flashed in her mind of meeting a witch who called herself Monica, a witch who had offered to give her back her hard-lost humanity.

But why had the witch —

"Do you usually sleep outside in trees?"

Startled awake, Jessica sat up too quickly and almost fell from her perch. Alex was the one who had spoken. He was sitting, completely at home, on another branch.

"Couldn't you rustle some leaves next time?" she grumped, though she felt herself beginning to smile at her odd but welcome visitor. "I nearly fell out of the tree. How'd you get up here without my hearing you?"

"I flew."

Jessica just shook her head.

"Well, if you don't like it, I'll get down." Alex jumped from the branch and landed gracefully, like a cat. Jessica followed more slowly, having no desire to break an ankle by showing off. They walked aimlessly through the darkened woods as they spoke.

"Don't you live somewhere? Or do you just follow me around all day?" Before, she had asked him a similar question as a joke, but this time she truly wanted an answer. It seemed a bit too much of a coincidence that he was out here tonight.

"I *live* nowhere," Alex answered, his voice serious despite the hint of teasing she could see in his eyes, "and it isn't day."

Jessica shook her head again as she realized there was no way to get a straight answer from him.

As she contemplated this fact, she noticed a design on his right wrist, which was only visible because his sleeve had slipped up when he had leapt from the tree.

"What's that?" she asked, pointing to the tattoo.

Alex rolled up his sleeve to reveal the entire design: a black wolf with golden eyes and white fangs stalked across his wrist. Jessica knew this beast; it was Fenris, the giant wolf who swallowed the sun in Norse mythology. Aubrey had the same design on *his* right wrist.

She took a deep breath to keep herself from speaking until her thoughts were under control.

This could not possibly be a coincidence.

Over the past day, she had struggled to come up with an explanation—besides the impossible one that Alex *was* Aubrey—that would account for all the similarities between the two of them. Now a stunningly obvious scenario at last occurred to her: Alex was a fan of Ash Night. Aubrey was described down to the last detail in *Tiger, Tiger.* What would stop someone, if he was so inclined, from getting black contact lenses, a matching pendant, and replicas of Aubrey's tattoos?

But before Jessica could comment on Alex's tattoo, he asked her, "What are you doing out here so late at night?"

"I couldn't sleep," she answered, still unnerved. "You?"

"Maybe I *am* stalking you," he teased.

"Well, then I'm flattered," she joked back, though the light words masked more serious thoughts. If her theory about his fascination with Aubrey the vampire proved true, how far might he take this role-playing game of his?

She began walking in the general direction of her house, and he walked with her. Their conversation fell into silence.

"You're quiet suddenly," Jessica observed. They were within sight of her house, and she had stopped walking to look at him. "What are you thinking about?"

Alex sighed. "Nothing you would care to know."

"Why don't you tell me, and let me be the judge of that?" she pressed.

"Blood and death and people who know too much," he answered, his voice more tired than threatening. "Go inside, Ash Night. I'll speak to you another time."

He walked away silently, not giving Jessica a chance to respond. By the time her mind had processed his words, he was out of sight.

Her anger rose again for an instant, in reaction to the fact that yet another person had somehow discovered who Ash Night was.

However, the anger was quashed by a prospect that was intriguing, yet frightening. If he was Aubrey, and vampires did exist, and he and his kind knew who she was . . . her life could end up being a great deal shorter than she had intended.

CHAPTER 14

"HOW CUTE," Fala spat, approaching Aubrey as he entered Las Noches. "How disgustingly cute."

"Excuse me?"

Fala laughed, a biting sound that told anyone within hearing to beware. "Do you honestly think I haven't been keeping my eye on the author, after all the trouble she's been causing? And you've been out there practically *flirting* with her!"

For a moment Aubrey hesitated, fighting an urge to check on Jessica and make sure Fala hadn't harmed her after he had left.

"Leave Jessica alone," he commanded, his voice hard. It wasn't wise to show any attachment to a human, but he refused to let Fala harm the girl.

"What is it about this human?" Fala sneered. "Aubrey the almighty, the hunter, the warrior, who feels nothing but contempt for anything mortal . . . If I didn't know better, I'd say you were attracted to her."

He laughed in answer to her taunt, which she had obviously hoped would bother him more. "You've made up my reason, Fala. What's *your* interest in her? Fala, the child who has been abused and hunted by almost every immortal creature on Earth, the coward who wants power without risk, the fake goddess . . ." He paused and watched the rage flicker through her eyes in response to his references to her humiliating past—the past Ash Night knew all too well. "If I didn't know better, I'd say you were jealous."

Aubrey knew this last accusation was ridiculous. Fala hated him far too much to be jealous of his attraction to anyone, much less a human. But the expression on her face as he said those last words was priceless.

"You vain, arrogant, human-loving *idiot*," Fala snarled. Then she disappeared before he had a chance to retaliate.

Aubrey ignored her words and chuckled

as he wandered over to the bar. He wasn't worried about Jessica for the moment. Had Fala actually killed her, she would have made it clear that she had done so. She would have insisted on sharing every bloody detail with him.

CHAPTER 15

CARYN RASHIDA WAITED inside the front door as Anne Allodola went to wake her daughter. Caryn ran over possible scenarios in her mind for the hundredth time.

"She'll be down in just a moment," Ms. Allodola said as she returned.

Caryn nodded nervously. She had made up her mind, and this time she would not let Jessica's frosty putdowns turn her away. Of course, waking her up might not have been a good idea, but how was she to know that Jessica would still be sleeping? It was almost noon.

When Jessica finally came downstairs, Caryn could instantly tell that she was in for a challenge. Jessica's aura hummed with annoyance and anger, as well as some confusion. As soon as she saw Caryn, the emotions found an outlet.

"What the hell do *you* want?" Jessica snapped.

Caryn flinched slightly. "I need to talk to you, Jessica."

"About what?"

"Alex."

Jessica's eyes narrowed as soon as Caryn said the name, and she stopped trying to herd Caryn out the door.

"What about Alex?" Jessica asked carefully. When Caryn looked toward the kitchen, where Anne was not-so-subtly eavesdropping, Jessica sighed. "Come upstairs. We can talk in my room."

Caryn hesitated at the doorway to Jessica's room, which was threateningly dark. There was no light besides the glow that came from a red Lava lamp on the shelf. Jessica removed the lamp's bottle so that the light shone pure white, but that only served to illuminate the room's gloomy monochrome.

"This is your room?" Caryn asked before she could think not to. She noticed one lonely hint of color: a violet pillow on the corner of the bed, half lost beneath the black comforter. She wondered how Jessica would react if she told her that violet was the color of humanity.

Caryn had a sudden, irrational desire to rescue the pillow from the blackness. That much she could do easily. Unlike Jessica, the pillow would not fight her.

"Say what you came to say, Caryn," Jessica growled.

Caryn went over the million different scripts she had prepared to tell Jessica the truth, then discarded them all. She walked to the shelf and sifted through the rough manuscripts until she found Jessica's copy of *Dark Flame.*

"I've heard about this," she said. Most of the world—excluding the humans—had heard of Ash Night's *Dark Flame.*

Jessica frowned, and Caryn could tell she was trying to make sense of the comment. Before she could formulate an answer, Caryn continued.

"How did you . . . get the idea for that book? And *Tiger, Tiger?*" she asked.

Jessica laughed, appearing shocked by the ordinariness of the question. "You came here to ask me how I get my *ideas?*"

Caryn took a deep breath to steady herself. "Not entirely." Her next words came out in a rush. "I wanted to ask if you knew they were true."

Jessica's expression was suddenly drained of its amusement.

"Get out, Caryn," she ordered coldly.

Caryn took a step back from Jessica's sudden vehemence. *Denial,* she reasoned. Jessica knew the truth but refused to accept it. It made perfect sense that she would fight back against anyone who attempted to convince her of what she was desperately trying to ignore.

Caryn inhaled deeply when she realized that she'd been holding her breath for the past few seconds.

"What do you know about Alex?" Caryn pressed. Jessica was exceptionally strong. When forced to see the truth, she would be able to accept it. If only Caryn knew how to convince her!

"I said, get out of my room," Jessica repeated.

"Will you think about what I said?" Beyond that simple request, Caryn was out of ideas. "Please?"

"If you'll leave." The answer was little more than a growl.

Caryn reached into her pocket and pulled out the letter she had written earlier, after several drafts. She held it out to Jessica, who snatched it from her hand.

"Happy now?" Jessica snapped.

Jessica's rampaging emotions were starting to make Caryn dizzy, so she nodded meekly and hurried out of the room. As she paused in the hallway, wishing she could think of some way to reason with Jessica, she heard the lock turn in the door. A few moments later loud music began to spill into the hall.

CHAPTER 16

JESSICA SPRAWLED across her bed with mindless noise blaring in her ears and tried to reason things out.

Caryn was playing with her. She knew the Rashidas and Alex had some relationship; they hated each other too much to be perfect strangers. For all she knew, Alex and Caryn used to date. Now they had ganged up to play a game of "let's mess with the author's mind."

It was cleverly done, she admitted reluctantly. Alex's portrayal of Aubrey was perfect. She wondered who Caryn was trying to be. If it was a game, it was well practiced and planned between them.

There is no if, she scolded herself. *Vampires do not exist!*

Jessica had no love of mind games, especially ones played by childish idiots like Caryn. She wondered if Caryn realized just how little sense of humor Jessica had when it came to her books.

Frustrated, she opened the letter that Caryn had handed her and scanned it quickly.

Then she read it again, more slowly, and then a third time.

Jessica —

I realize how confused you must be now. I don't know how to explain to you that everything you are thinking right now is true. I can't imagine how you got involved in this world; all I know is that what you write puts you in danger.

With your permission, I will try to help you, but I can't do anything unless you ask me to. I'm not a fighter, but I know others who are. If you will let me, I will ask them for help.

Stay away from Aubrey, away from all of them. Stop writing your books about them. Maybe then they will not see the

*need to destroy you. You well know how
dangerous they are. Please, be careful.*

Blessed be,
Caryn Smoke
Daughter of Macht

*I am signing with my true name now. I
don't wish to lie to you as all the others
would.*

"What is going on here?" Jessica asked
the black walls. They said nothing—they
rarely did, though when she was dead tired
they sometimes made an exception.

Everyone who had read Ash Night's first
book knew who Aubrey was—what he
looked like, where he was from, how he
spoke, and how he thought. The two books
that had gone through her editor's office
revealed the dark corners of Aubrey's past
and his present, and had reached into the
wider vampiric world to show its customs
and politics.

Never once had these books mentioned
the Smoke line of witches or their immortal
mother, Macht, whom Caryn had so casually referenced in her letter.

Without conscious thought, Jessica picked up one of the manuscripts that had been sitting on her shelf for months now. Though she hadn't read the novel since she had written it, she remembered the characters inside. The story was set years earlier; the witches mentioned in it would be Caryn's distant ancestors. Jessica knew, through the eyes of her vampiric characters, all about the Smoke line. But *only* she should have known, because the manuscript had been read by no one else. The fine layer of dust on the binder was proof that no one had picked it up recently. There was no way Caryn could ever have read it.

The girl's words echoed in Jessica's mind: *What if it was all real? If Ash Night's vampires actually existed?*

And more recently: *I wanted to ask if you knew they were true.*

Though Jessica hadn't delved too far into the world of the Smoke witches, simply because they were of little interest to her vampires, she knew their basic beliefs. If a Smoke witch was aware that someone was in danger, it was that witch's duty to protect him or her.

If it was true, Jessica was certainly in danger.

If they were all real . . .

If Aubrey existed, and Jessica had met him, then why was she still alive? He had no scruples about killing, and she had shown the world every weak moment of his past. Yet when she mentally replayed her conversations with him, there was no sense of threat. He seemed more to be flirting with her than hunting her.

She needed to know if it was true. She knew these characters better than she knew even Anne. They had been her thoughts and life for years. If there was the slightest chance that they were real, she needed to know.

She needed proof, and to get that, she needed to see for herself.

CHAPTER 17

IN JESSICA'S NOVELS, New Mayhem was the base of vampiric power in the United States. The town, which was hidden from the human world, was home to the ruling class of vampires—Silver's line, including Aubrey. Their presence had given it a flavor of darkness that Jessica knew she would recognize if she saw it.

She searched through her manuscripts and found various clues to the location of New Mayhem, which was Ramsa's secret neighbor. She had always assumed that she had located New Mayhem near Ramsa out of familiarity, but perhaps instead some trick of the vampiric world had caused *her* to be located *here*.

One of her manuscripts, at this point untitled, caught her eye. The story was that of Kaei, the mostly human bartender at the vampire nightclub Las Noches. Kaei had been born and raised in the original town of Mayhem. She had been responsible for the fire that had nearly leveled the town three hundred years earlier, and in punishment had been blood-bonded to Jager. Kaei was not a vampire, but she would not age as long as Jager was alive.

After that episode, the witches had mostly believed that Mayhem was gone forever. When New Mayhem was built, the mortal Macht witches and the immortal Tristes had not been informed. The vampire hunters had not known about New Mayhem.

Until *Tiger, Tiger* had revealed its existence. Jessica silently contemplated this latest realization as she walked down the darkened road toward the town that might or might not be there.

The walk was longer than she would have liked, but not painfully so. Perhaps three miles went by before Jessica noticed a narrow, unnamed path off to the side of the road. Normally she would not have given the path a second glance after all the nearly identical driveways she had passed, but tonight she saw beside it the sign she had been looking for: a rosebush, which climbed the base of an oak tree.

The last of the blooms was still on the bush, and when she stepped near it, Jessica saw that the flower was black. For more than five hundred years, the vampires had used a black rose as their symbol.

She knelt for a moment, her fingers resting on the silky petals of the rose as she tried to calm her breathing. She no longer needed to see the town to convince herself that everything was true; though her mind might still protest, she believed despite it. Now there was a more compelling reason for her to follow the path. It would lead her home. She had seen New Mayhem through dozens of views but had never even glimpsed it with her own eyes, yet as she walked, she had the strangest sensation that she was finally heading home.

The path went on for what seemed an interminable time. Walking down that path was a test of courage that most people would have failed. The darkness was oppressive, and the forest was unnaturally silent. The isolation pressed against her like a physical weight. Yet, unafraid, she welcomed the night and the loneliness like old friends.

The woods began to thin so gradually that Jessica hardly noticed the change until she saw the first building in New Mayhem. It was Nyeusigrube, which meant "den of shadows." Jessica knew the name well.

She leaned against the side of the building, her legs suddenly weak as the truth slugged her in the gut.

She was all but numb from shock, but not from denial. She believed; she had no choice but to believe.

The black rose had been the symbol of the vampires for more than five hundred years; that alone was daunting. But five hundred years might have been the blink of an eye to some of Ash Night's characters, and for a moment Jessica felt the weight of all the lives she had juggled in her books. Thousands of years' worth of love and hate and pain and pleasure had somehow been compressed into Jessica's subconscious mortal mind.

For a moment she wondered if she should just stay here instead of returning to her human world. She could disappear, as Mayhem had disappeared three hundred years before.

But as tempting as the world of Ash Night might be, Jessica knew that a human in New Mayhem was seen as a lower being. In comparison to the vampires, mortals were weak, foolish children. Jessica's pride would not allow her to be submissive to these characters whose every weakness she had written about.

However, there was no way for her to simply turn back and ignore what she knew. Instead, she had an irrational desire—no, a *need*—to see the creatures of her novels.

In a daze, she made her way to the heart of New Mayhem, not hesitating to push open the door and enter the chaos known as Las Noches.

Jessica couldn't tell if it was the room or her head that was spinning. Her reflection was distorted wildly by the shattered mirrors, and the black wooden furniture seemed to dance in the moving lights.

As she stood just inside the door, she was hit by such a strong sense of recognition that she reeled back a step. She knew almost everyone in the room.

A slender, dark-skinned woman leaned against the bar. She lifted the crystal glass she held and sipped from it a viscous red liquid that Jessica had no desire to identify. She did recognize the vampire, though: it was Fala.

Fala looked up, and her black eyes immediately fell on the human author with distaste.

Welcome to my world. Fala's icy voice echoed through Jessica's mind, sending a chill down her spine. *Or is it your world?*

Jessica knew she was being tested, but she only shook her head. *It isn't mine,* she thought in answer, knowing Fala would hear her.

Damn right. The ancient vampire lifted her glass as if to propose a toast. *To knowledge, and to pain.*

Understanding the threat, Jessica turned away and left quickly. She had no wish to engage in any kind of confrontation with Fala.

Outside Las Noches she stopped and leaned against the cool wall, waiting for her dizziness to subside. But after a minute or so, she forced herself to move. Though vampires were not allowed to kill humans inside New Mayhem, Jessica doubted that anyone would object to Fala's making an exception in the case of the author Ash Night.

CHAPTER 18

JESSICA WAS BARELY OUT of New Mayhem, still in the woods that surrounded the single path back to the human world, when she heard the rustle of leaves behind her.

Spinning to face the potential threat, she let out a tight breath as she saw Aubrey.

He had murdered any illusion of the human Alex Remington. The golden pendant had been replaced by a spiked dog collar, and he was wearing a black T-shirt that hugged his form and showed off the many designs on his arms: Fenris on the right wrist, and Echidna, the Greek mother of all monsters, high on his left arm. The Norse world serpent was wrapped around his left wrist, and a new design had recently been added: Cerberus, the three-headed dog who guarded the gates of Hades. The World Serpent was partially covered by a black leather knife sheath, which held the silver knife Aubrey had taken from a vampire hunter a few thousand years earlier.

His hair was slightly tousled, as if he'd been running, and a few strands fell across his face.

Looking at him now, Jessica couldn't imagine how she had ever mistaken him for a human. But illusion was Aubrey's art. And it was simple to fool people who expected nothing else.

For the moment, Aubrey appeared to be exactly what he was: stunning, mischievous, and completely deadly all at once. She could feel the aura of power that hung about him, a tangible sensation like a cool pocket in the still night air. Here, outside the confines of the sunlit world, Aubrey was every inch the dark, seductive vampire of popular myth.

"Leaving so soon?" he asked, glancing for a moment back at New Mayhem.

Jessica's thoughts turned to Fala. "I might have stayed longer, but the threats were a bit discouraging." Her tone was light, despite the truth in her words. She had always preferred sarcasm and jokes to fear and pleading.

"Many are calling for your blood," Aubrey answered seriously, "but there are actually very few of my kind who would dare to kill you."

She could not read the emotion in his face as he spoke those words, but there was something there, just beneath the surface — a meaning she was missing. However, she knew the danger of holding a vampire's gaze, so she didn't try to read the truth in his eyes as she otherwise might have done.

Instead she stepped forward, on the offensive. She was tired of this guessing. "I suppose you're one of the few," she said, but somehow the words didn't ring true.

Aubrey's voice when he answered was soft. "I'm one of the reasons they wouldn't dare."

"And why is that?" she pressed, moving still closer.

He didn't respond, but instead watched her, the look in his eyes disconcertingly intense.

"I don't like being toyed with, Aubrey," Jessica announced, forcing her thoughts back into focus. "If you or anyone else is planning to kill me, then get on with it. I have better things to do than wait for you to act."

Aubrey looked vaguely amused, but at the same time she could tell he was becoming defensive. She knew he wasn't used to hearing any human speak to him boldly. Still, he raised an eyebrow, inviting her to continue.

She answered by slapping him, hard enough that his head snapped to the side and her palm stung.

The act had not been planned. Impatience and anger and confusion had been rising in her system for too long and had simply reached their zenith.

She had wanted him to take her seriously, and now he would. The expression on his face had changed to pure shock. Jessica knew that he would kill most humans for less, but right now she was too stirred up to feel afraid.

CHAPTER 19

AUBREY'S AGITATION rivaled Jessica's. He had never been more surprised by a human than he was at this moment. Despite the fact that she had just committed a shockingly reckless act, the expression on her face was utterly fearless.

She stepped forward again, aggressive. Her ebony hair tumbled down past her shoulders like a waterfall of midnight.

"Well? What does your kind want with me?" she demanded. "Why am I not dead already?"

"That seems to be a point of dispute," he answered, trying to keep his voice nonchalant.

"You're the only one here. What's stopping you?" she challenged, meeting his gaze without the slightest hesitation.

She stood in front of him, arms across her chest, head held high as if she was looking down at him, black hair shaken back from her face, green eyes strong and defiant. Her entire stance screamed "predator."

A predatory mind-set was something one was or was not born with. Even some vampires still acted like prey. Jessica acted as if she was afraid of nothing.

"Well?" she said, stepping forward again. She was intentionally invading his space, forcing him to react.

"What do you want from me?" Aubrey asked finally. Her mind was a blank to him at the moment. Despite all the years he had spent learning to manipulate every situation, he had no idea what she wanted him to do.

"I know as much about your kind as you do," Jessica said. "Probably more. I've written it all down and allowed other humans to read it. I've even told them about the only fight you've ever really lost in your life. And I'm not going to stop writing, no matter how many times your kind threatens me with death. I'm not afraid of the inevitable." She took one more step forward so that she was all but spitting her words in his face. "What do you want to do about it?"

Jessica looked into his eyes fearlessly. She stood so close that he could feel her breath, but he held his ground, his arms motionless at his sides. They were locked into a challenge that was like a confrontation between two wild cats, each refusing to be the first to look away.

Aubrey was struck by the color of her eyes: a perfect green he had never before seen in any human — somehow impossibly deep. For a moment he experienced the disorientation that he knew his own gaze had so often caused.

His shock was now complete. Jessica had looked into his eyes brazenly, and *he* had been the one caught.

He blinked once, trying to clear his mind, and his thoughts returned to her question.

Over the past few days, he had occasionally wanted to throttle her for her unrealized knowledge and stubborn innocence, and he had once or twice entertained the idea of simply sinking his teeth into that fair and tender throat, which the outfit she wore tonight displayed so well. Most often, though, he had had the urge to do exactly what he wanted to do right now.

"What do I want to do about it?" he mused aloud.

Jessica gasped as he wrapped an arm around her waist and pulled her forward to close the few remaining inches between them. Before she could react, he caught her lips with his own. The kiss was strong but over quickly, and then he willed himself away.

CHAPTER 20

JESSICA STOOD STUNNED for a few minutes after Aubrey had disappeared; then she flopped back against a tree and tried to make sense of the world.

She had thought she was facing death tonight. She had resolved to face it unflinchingly. Instead ...

The scene replayed in her mind, frame by frame. The stillness while she had waited for Aubrey to answer her challenge. The vision of him standing there like a creature formed from the very breath of night.

Finally there had been the brief sensation of his lips on hers, over before she could respond, but potent enough to make every thought in her mind lose its cohesiveness.

If he had simply killed her, she would have understood. But this . . . this she could not explain.

The night air did nothing to cool her thoughts as she headed home, finally slipping into the house at nearly one in the morning.

Sleep eluded her, so she paced in her room for nearly an hour before turning on the computer with the hope of losing herself in her writing. Sometime shortly before sunrise, exhaustion finally claimed her restless mind. She dreamed.

For a few moments, Jazlyn didn't know what had happened or who she was. She had vague memories of meeting a witch who called herself Monica Smoke, a witch who offered to give her back her hard-lost humanity.

But why had the witch made this offer? Why had Jazlyn accepted? Everything was so faint in her mind. Monica had been afraid to even speak to Jazlyn. Why had she given back the life that Jazlyn had willingly tossed away?

Jazlyn's mind drifted back to the night she had died.

She had known for years the black-haired, green-eyed creature who called himself Siete, and she had been offered immortality often. She had refused every time. After all, she was twenty-five, she had a husband, and life was perfect.

Siete had twice changed humans against their wills, and both times the result had been disastrous, so he accepted Jazlyn's refusals with good grace.

Then everything had changed. Carl, the love of her life, her husband for three years, was hit by a drunk driver. He died in a hospital bed while she wept in the waiting room.

Her parents had both passed away several years before, and her friends were few and far between. There was no shoulder she could cry on. The only one who was there for her was the immortal Siete.

She still said no. Immortality was not what she wanted. Immortality without Carl was meaningless. She wanted only to be left alone and given time to grieve. Even this was denied her —

A knock on the door woke Jessica.

She lifted her head from the desktop and rubbed her eyes as she heard Anne call her name. According to Jessica's computer, it was now just past ten in the morning.

Sleeping at her desk for five hours had left

her with some kinks in her neck. She stood and stretched, then shut down her computer and opened the door to answer Anne.

Anne, wearing her Sunday best, had been about to knock on Jessica's door again.

"Are you running early or is my clock wrong?" Jessica asked, confused as to why Anne was all dressed up for church when she didn't need to leave for another hour.

"I told Hasana Rashida I'd meet up with her for a coffee before the service," Anne explained. "Hasana is your friend Caryn's mother. Have you met her?"

Jessica nodded once and managed not to add anything that might offend Anne.

"Caryn will be with us, if you'd like to come," Anne added hopefully. She offered the invitation every week, though Jessica never accepted.

Part of Jessica's dream gnawed at her: Monica *Smoke*. If anyone would know about Jazlyn, Monica's relatives would.

However, she had no desire to make small talk with Caryn and Hasana, so she declined the offer, deciding instead to speak with one of them outside the church. She took a shower and dressed slowly while Anne gathered her belongings and left the house.

Walking, Jessica reached the church about fifteen minutes before the service was scheduled to start. She waited at the corner of the building as Hasana, Caryn, and Anne approached, laughing. She didn't try to get their attention, and vaguely realized that she reminded herself of one of her characters, stalking prey.

As Hasana and Anne became lost in the crowd near the church doors, Jessica caught Caryn's arm.

"Caryn, I need to talk to you," she said in a hushed tone.

The girl jumped a bit but seemed to relax when she saw who had grabbed her. They slipped out of the group and into a less crowded area of the churchyard.

"About?" Caryn asked.

But before Jessica could answer, Caryn gasped. Her face froze in a look of horror as she pointed toward the side wall of the church.

It took Jessica a few moments to register what Caryn was seeing. The second she did, she bounded across the yard—toward Anne and the vampire who had her in his grasp.

Jessica didn't recognize the vampire, which she supposed was a good sign; if she hadn't written about him, he probably wasn't very strong. She was counting on that fact.

Tearing the vampire away from Anne, she slammed her fist into his jaw before he could even figure out what was happening. Anne stumbled back against the wall, and Caryn and Hasana, from opposite ends of the churchyard, hurried to her side. The rest of the churchgoers, clearly under the mind control of the vampire, continued to chat and make their way cheerfully into the building.

Before Jessica had a chance to check on Anne, the vampire turned and hit her hard enough that she found herself on the ground, her head spinning.

The vampire looked nervously from the witches and Anne to the group of people near the doors of the church, and Jessica could all but see his thoughts. If Caryn and Hasana interfered, he wouldn't be able to keep his control over the crowd, and this confrontation would get even messier.

Then he looked at Jessica, staring fiercely at her for one long moment. She tried to stand but couldn't find her balance; he had probably given her a concussion with that little love tap. She braced herself for his next strike. But he was gone.

Why had he left when he could have killed her in an instant? Suddenly last night's conversation popped back into her head.

There are actually very few of my kind who would dare to kill you.

I suppose you're one of the few.

I'm one of the reasons they wouldn't dare.

"Thank you, Aubrey," she said softly.

Caryn moved from Anne's side to Jessica's. Her face was pale, and she said nothing for a moment.

Jessica tried again to stand, and a wave of blackness passed over her vision. Caryn put a hand on her arm to help her up, then gently touched the side of Jessica's head where the vampire had hit her.

Jessica jerked back when she felt the warm wave of energy that flowed out of Caryn.

"Jessica—"

"I'm fine," she snapped, infuriated by her own weakness. She refused to accept help from Caryn.

But as she pulled away, she forced herself to add, "Thank you." The dizziness was gone completely.

As her thoughts focused, Jessica asked, "What about Anne?"

Caryn looked at her mother, who just shook her head.

Jessica's legs went out from under her.

"Jessica, I'm sorry . . ." Hasana was speaking, but Jessica hardly heard the words.

Caryn tried to take her hand, but she shook it off and went to Anne's side.

Anne was pale, but Jessica could tell that it wasn't blood loss that had killed her. The vampire hadn't had the time, so instead he had broken her neck.

She balled her hands into fists, so tightly that her nails drew blood from her palms. Why had he killed her? He had done so intentionally, not just to feed.

As she took the dead woman's hand, Jessica saw a piece of paper tucked into Anne's grip. Pulling it out, she needed to read no more than the first line before she recognized it as a page from the *Dark Flame* manuscript. It was a page on which Fala was described.

Scrawled on the back, in sharp black ink, were four words: *Stay in your place.*

Jessica found herself shaking with anger — at the nameless vampire who had killed

Anne, and especially at Fala, who must have put him up to it.

Fala would never have been able to convince one of her kind to go directly against Aubrey, even if for some reason she hadn't wanted to kill Jessica with her own hands. But Anne was free and defenseless prey.

Hasana put a hand on Jessica's shoulder. "Come, Jessica. There are other people to deal with this. You don't need to stay here."

Jessica shrugged out of Hasana's grip, still looking at the only human who had ever bothered to care for her.

CHAPTER 21

AUBREY PACED IN HIS ROOM, as he'd done shortly after he'd first met Jessica Allodola, trying to reason out his emotions. It was nearly noon, and he was still awake; that alone was enough to make him irritable. Coupled with his confusion about last night's confrontation, he was very much in the mood to pick a fight.

She had stared him down. He couldn't help respecting her for it. Not to mention her all-but-suicidal challenge —

Not so suicidal, he reminded himself, interrupting his own thought. *She won, after all.*

Jessica was like a sand viper: beautiful,

not apparently formidable, but fearless and deadly poisonous.

"Damn you, Fala," he whispered as the vampire's taunt echoed in his head: *If I didn't know better, I'd say you were attracted to her.* "Why aren't you ever wrong?"

Of course, there was more than the physical attraction Fala had speculated about. The actuality was far more dangerous both to his own position—as was any emotional attachment to a human—and to Jessica if any of his many enemies guessed the truth.

Furious with himself for letting this girl get under his skin, he went into Las Noches, where he was immediately intercepted by Fala herself. Apparently he wasn't the only one who couldn't sleep this morning.

"You didn't kill her," Fala accused as soon as she saw him. "She was strutting around our land as if she owned it, practically begging for death, and *you didn't kill her.*"

"No, I didn't," he answered in a growl.

"Aubrey—"

"What is your obsession with killing this one human?" he snapped.

"She's a threat," Fala answered calmly, obviously pleased by how close he was to losing his control. She looked almost amused, which made him wary. Fala was clever; she was the one most likely to figure out his feelings toward Jessica.

"And how is that?" he argued. "Just because she writes about things that almost every vampire in the world already knows and most mortals disregard as fiction?"

"*Most* is the key word there, Aubrey," Fala chided. "Have you forgotten those not-quite-insignificant mortals called vampire hunters? Kala is *dead*, Aubrey. Your blood sister, Ather's second fledgling. And she was run through by a witch practically on the front steps of Las Noches. That witch wouldn't even have known this place *existed* if it hadn't been for Ash Night."

"Jessica had nothing to do with Dominique Vida's finding Las Noches," Aubrey argued. "And since when are you afraid of vampire hunters?"

Fala let out a half-curse, half-scream as she began to lose her temper. "What is she going to write next, Aubrey? The only reason she's gotten this far is because *you're* protecting her. Fine, you've established your power. Now why don't you just *kill* her?"

He turned away from her, refusing to answer.

Behind him Fala snickered. "It's true, isn't it? You're attracted to her. I was right all along."

Aubrey reeled back around as her words hit him.

"She's a good-looking young woman, I'll admit," Fala continued. "But that isn't the issue, is it? You've —"

"Fala," he warned, his voice dangerous.

"It isn't that unusual, you know," she continued, sounding even more amused. "It's our line's curse, you could say. *Love.*" She spat the word as if it was some kind of insect.

Finally Aubrey's voice returned. "No truer than in your case. Isn't that *curse,* as you put it, why you're here? Isn't that why Jager changed you in the first place?" Jager and Fala had met while she'd been awaiting death in one of the sandy cells of ancient Egypt. He had changed her the same day. It was still obvious to any idiot how fond they were of each other.

Fala started to retaliate, but he continued. "Not to mention Moira. It seems that the awful, infectious disease has hit you several times." Fala's eyes narrowed at the mention of her beloved Moira.

Then she sighed. "Look what she's done to you, Aubrey," she said, her voice soft, almost sympathetic. "Kill her . . . or change her. If you're really so fond of her, give her your blood. Do whatever you want with her, but *stop* her." She paused, suddenly unnerved. "You know, Silver once gave Jager this same advice—about Kaei."

Aubrey remembered the argument, which had occurred shortly after Kaei had sliced open Silver's arm and shortly before she had set fire to most of Mayhem.

"I hardly think that's relevant," Aubrey answered. "Jessica certainly isn't going to —"

"I think it's very relevant," Fala interrupted. "Jager refused to kill her."

CHAPTER 22

HASANA HAD INSISTED that Jessica go home with them, instead of staying with the police and the medical units. No matter what her personal feelings toward Jessica, Hasana was still a mother, and Jessica could see the motherly care in everything she did.

Jessica refused at first to go anywhere with the Smoke family, but she gave in when Hasana had Caryn go fetch her belongings—including her computer. At least they understood that she wouldn't go anywhere without a way to write.

Her anger over Anne's death had been replaced by a dismal apathy so overpowering that when she was confronted, the moment she stepped through the Rashidas' door, by Dominique Vida, she didn't even bother to make a biting response.

Dominique, despite her classic beauty, had all the social skills and warmth of an icicle. The air near her hummed with strictly controlled energy. Perhaps the apathy was helpful; otherwise, Jessica might have been tempted to kill Dominique on the spot.

Unlike the Smoke line, Jessica knew Dominique and her kin well. Dominique had murdered so many of the vampires that Jessica had known and cared for that the girl had developed a deep hatred for the witch before she had even met her.

Only when Caryn put a hand on her shoulder did Jessica realize that she was glaring death in Dominique's direction. The vampire hunter was fully returning the glare.

"What is *she* doing here?" Dominique demanded.

Caryn took the initiative to lead Jessica away and into a guest room while Hasana dealt with Dominique's questions.

"You should get some rest," Caryn suggested, trying to pull Jessica out of her inner world of death and pain and hatred.

"Only if there's a way to make sure no one

kills me in my sleep," Jessica answered, looking out the door as if Dominique might walk down the hall any moment.

Caryn looked horrified. "She wouldn't . . ." She trailed off. "Why would she want to hurt you?"

Jessica shrugged. That question had an easy answer at least. "Because I can't help hating her," she answered truthfully. "And because she knows I would rather be a vampire than risk being their prey." Jessica thought back to poor Anne, who was just as dead no matter how many vampires Dominique and her kin had killed.

"I'll keep that in mind," answered Dominique, who had just entered the room, with Hasana behind her. Caryn paled.

"No one is going to hurt anyone in my household," Hasana said firmly. "Jessica, you don't know what you're saying right now —"

"She knows," Dominique interrupted. Turning to Jessica, she said bluntly, "If you'd rather be with them, then go. I won't stop you. But if you choose their side, then I won't protect you, either."

"I don't need your protection," Jessica growled in answer.

"Jessica, please, get some rest," Hasana coaxed. "Dominique, leave the poor girl alone. Her mother was just murdered." She ushered Dominique out of the room. The hunter went willingly; she had said all she needed to say.

Jessica had no desire to sleep, and she told Caryn as much.

"You should try," Caryn answered. "It will help clear your mind."

Instead, Jessica began to pace.

Caryn caught her arm, and only a few seconds later, sleep enveloped her. Later the thought occurred to her that despite Caryn's usual passivity, she was still a strong witch. She had easily induced sleep in Jessica's strained mind.

Jazlyn said no. Immortality was not what she wanted. She wanted to be left alone and given time to grieve. Even this was denied her.

A week after Carl's death, Jazlyn learned that she was pregnant. Looking at her, no one would have been able to tell, but the tests had returned positive.

Why would the universe not leave her alone? She was only twenty-five, and she was a widow. How could she raise a child by herself? Carl's child de-

served better than what she, who was still in mourning, could provide.

A cruel God gave her this life.

The next time Siete visited, Jazlyn did not say no. She knew that whatever life she woke up in would not be the life she was leaving.

But any decision made out of desperation is later regretted. The world of eternal night and lawlessness was no better than the human world she had fled, yet Jazlyn had no more choices.

The years passed and faded, meaningless and empty. Often Jazlyn found herself remembering things like the beach on which Carl had proposed. She remembered being married outdoors and honeymooning in France.

Tears came frequently. This was not what she had wanted at all.

Just past Valentine's Day 1983, Jazlyn visited Carl's grave for the first time since his funeral. She brushed off the thin layer of snow and read the stone for the first time: "Carl Raisa, 1932–1960. 'I shall smile from Heaven upon those I love. My death is not my end, and in Heaven shall I meet my beloved again.'"

But he wouldn't, because she was never going to reach Heaven. Her kind was evil; she had killed so many times·to sate the bloodlust that she would never be forgiven.

Jazlyn lay weeping in the snowy graveyard that Valentine's night, wondering why the world had chosen her to torment.

That was where the witch who called herself Monica Smoke had found her—weeping there for the one she loved. Monica was the first one in more than twenty years who offered her a shoulder to cry on. Then she heard the story and gave Jazlyn the one thing she had thought could never be returned: her life.

CHAPTER 23

As soon as she woke, Jessica sought out her hostesses. Avoiding Dominique Vida, she quickly found Caryn in her room.

"Do you know of anyone in your line called Monica?" she demanded, closing the door behind her.

"Yes," Caryn said after a moment of hesitation. "She was my aunt, my mother's sister."

"Was?"

"She died. Mother never told me how." Caryn frowned. "Why, Jessica. What's wrong?"

Jessica didn't answer, her mind focused on her own questions. "Have you ever heard of someone called Jazlyn Raisa?" Jessica was determined to understand her own birth, even if that was the only part of her life she did understand.

"Jazlyn Raisa . . . No. But maybe my mother would."

Jessica nodded quickly.

"Jessica, what is this about?"

She shook off the question, impatient to find Hasana and hear the truth.

As Jessica entered the kitchen, Hasana looked up from whatever she was cooking. She seemed to sense Jessica's urgency.

"Jessica, do you need something?"

"Jazlyn Raisa," Jessica answered without prelude. "I want to know about her."

Hasana's face betrayed her mistrust. She paused, taking a breath, and then asked, "What do you know about Raisa?"

"She was a vampire, a direct fledgling of Siete," Jessica answered. "And your sister offered to give her back her life."

Hasana's eyes narrowed. "I didn't believe it was possible, but Monica insisted she could do it. She died trying, and I heard nothing more about it."

"She succeeded," Jessica filled in.

"Raisa didn't deserve it," Hasana growled.

"If you know so much, why are you asking me?"

"Jazlyn was pregnant when Siete changed her," Jessica explained, and she saw shock fill Hasana's expression. "I want to know what would have happened to the child when Jazlyn became human again."

The idea seemed far-fetched. Though Jessica knew plenty about her vampires, she knew nothing about anyone who had ever become human again besides what her dreams had told of Jazlyn. Only a witch would know if a baby carried in a vampiric womb would regain its life with its mother.

"I didn't know there was a child," Hasana whispered. "Now I understand. Monica wouldn't have risked her life to save a vampire. But a baby . . . Monica must have believed that it would survive."

"What happened to the child?" Jessica shouted. She had to force herself not to grab Hasana by the shoulders and try to shake the information from her.

"I didn't know there was one," Hasana repeated, shaking her head apologetically. Jessica turned away and returned to the room she'd been given, needing to think.

Her mother. The term brought a moment of pain. The woman who had raised her was dead; now she had been replaced by a phantom who had never wanted Jessica. Jazlyn Raisa.

Jessica paced softly in her room, trying to organize her thoughts.

Siete was the first of the vampires. He was ancient, even compared to Fala and Jager and Silver, and his mind was powerful enough that he could easily know everything that Jessica had written. His blood ran through her veins as surely as it had run through her mother's, and her link to him was no doubt as strong as the link he had with his fledglings. The difference was that she was human and had no shields against his mind. So when she slept or simply drifted, she shared his dreams and his thoughts.

The puzzle had come together finally.

Jessica's gaze fell on her computer. Without making a conscious decision to do so, she sat down and booted it up, wanting to hear the comforting hum.

The familiar compulsion struck her. But ignoring the book she had been working on, she began another, though she had no idea how this one was going to end.

> *The night is full of mystery. Even when the moon is brightest, secrets hide everywhere. Then the sun rises and its rays cast so many shadows that the day creates more illusion than all the veiled truth of the night.*

Several hours and many pages passed before the flow of thoughts ceased. Who, she wondered, would finish it if she died?

CHAPTER 24

NEEDING TO GET AWAY from the magic-choked atmosphere of the house, Jessica slipped out of her room and down the stairs.

"Where are you going, Jessica? I'm just about to serve dinner."

She froze, hearing Hasana's voice, and turned to see Dominique and Hasana standing together in the next room.

"I was planning to go for a walk, perhaps wander in the woods a bit," she answered. "Is there something wrong with that?"

Hasana sighed. "Jessica, do you really think you should be going out there alone?" Jessica could hear a hint of annoyance in her voice.

"Do *you* really think I can stay inside until Dominique has killed all the vampires?" Jessica snapped in return. She knew Hasana was trying to help, but she felt like a wolf caged in the shepherd's barn.

"I could at least deal with a few of them," Dominique said, watching Jessica as if for a reaction. "After a while, the others will probably decide you aren't worth the trouble."

"After you *murder* another dozen or so of them," Jessica choked out. She had a sudden, vivid image of Aubrey with Dominique's knife in his heart. She would not wish Dominique even upon Fala.

"It isn't murder to kill something that died thousands of years ago," Dominique argued. "Murder is what *they* do every night, when even you know they don't need to kill in order to feed. Murder is what they did yesterday to your mother."

Jessica took an involuntary step toward Dominique and felt the first warning strike from the hunter: a slight burning sensation on the surface of her skin, which flared for a moment and then faded.

Hasana put a hand on Dominique's arm to get her attention. "Dominique, I hardly think that comment was necessary."

Dominique sighed. "If she's going to be staying in this house with you and Caryn, then I need to know whose side she's on," she asserted. "Well, Jessica?"

"If it's a choice between you and them," Jessica spat in answer, "then I would choose the vampires any day. At least they don't preach the morality of their killing."

She spun away, trying to ignore the tension between her shoulders, where she expected any moment to feel the point of Dominique's knife.

CHAPTER 25

IT WAS NOT YET SUNSET when Jessica arrived, once again, at the doorway to Las Noches.

There were fewer people in the room than the last time, which was probably related to the fact that Fala and Aubrey were fighting near the bar.

They stopped in surprise as Jessica entered and began walking fearlessly toward them.

Fala recovered her wits first and slammed Aubrey back into the bar. The sickening crack of a broken bone reached Jessica's ears even above the music of Las

Noches, but she knew he would heal almost instantly.

However, Fala used Aubrey's moment of pain to whisper a threat into his ear. Jessica could only hear the end of it as she approached. *Either deal with it now, or I will.*

Fala left the club without giving Jessica a second glance.

Aubrey stretched, already recovered from Fala's attack. As he turned toward Jessica, she saw him check for the knife at his waist, then shake his head, seeming neither surprised nor concerned to find it gone.

"You're an idiot, you know that?" Aubrey said as Jessica approached. "We both are."

"How do you figure that?" Jessica asked. She ignored the fight that she had just witnessed; she knew she was probably the reason behind it.

Parched from the walk in the sunlight, she considered trying to find something to drink in Las Noches's bar, but worried that she might knock herself out if she chose the wrong thing. While there was nothing in the bar that could kill a vampire, there was plenty that could damage a human.

"You know most of my kind is trying to kill you—particularly the one who just left—and still you come into New Mayhem at sunset," Aubrey answered dryly.

Jessica had to laugh at that. "My mother was killed yesterday beside a church in broad daylight. If any of your kind was really trying to kill me, it wouldn't matter where I was."

She decided that she could probably identify water if she saw it, so she rounded the bar to search.

"Are you trying to poison yourself?" Aubrey inquired, watching her.

"Oh, bite me," she taunted automatically, before the irony of the remark registered.

But Aubrey took her at her word. In a graceful movement, he wrapped a hand around the back of her neck and pulled her toward him.

"A tempting offer." He gently brushed the hollow of her throat with the thumb of his free hand as he spoke.

"You wouldn't."

He leaned down and she felt his lips at her neck. *It would never occur to you to be afraid, would it?* he silently asked.

If you wanted to kill me, you would have done so long ago. She projected the thought and knew that he could hear it.

Are you so sure?

No, she answered. *But if you bite me I'm going to bite back, and do you really want this crowd to see a human do that?* She was well aware that they had an attentive audience by now.

Is that what you *want?*

Jessica didn't quite understand Aubrey's question, but he must have sensed her confusion, because he added, *I did something similar to Ather, and we both know how that turned out.* Aubrey had been changed shortly after a fight with Ather. He had slit her throat when she had tried to feed on him. *Even Fala has suggested that I change you.*

You're right, you are *an idiot*, she commented in response. *And yes, that is what I want, which means you can't do it.*

Jessica was referring to the fact that Aubrey's line retained its power because every one of them fought. That struggle, as the blood was drained out, was what gave them their strength.

Yes, Jessica was more than willing to become one of their kind. Her hatred of Dominique had finally convinced her. But her readiness meant that she wouldn't fight, and her strength as a vampire would suffer. She would certainly be weaker than Fala. In essence, if Aubrey changed her now, it would be the same as his allowing Fala to kill her.

Aubrey knew all this as well, of course, so he released her and she stepped back casually, smoothing her shirt as if the confrontation had been normal. He reached past her, into the bar, and pulled out a bottle of water. She accepted it calmly and took a drink.

CHAPTER 26

WHAT WAS HE TO DO about the human called Jessica? Aubrey had had that thought before, and the answer was no more forthcoming than it had ever been.

Jessica had no idea how close she'd just come to having every drop of blood drained from her body. The feel of her pulse beneath his lips had almost broken even his self-control.

He needed to hunt, but he hesitated to leave her alone. Fala's threat was still fresh in his mind.

The decision was made for him as he heard a faint cry coming from just outside

the building. It was a distressed voice he
knew well: the voice of Kaei. That girl could
get herself into more scrapes in an hour than
most humans could accumulate in a year.

Nodding a silent goodbye to Jessica, he
quickly made his way to Kaei's side. She
could be a nuisance and worse to those who
treated her badly, and had caused more than
her fair share of trouble, but she was unwa-
veringly loyal to those she considered her
friends. Fala would probably not attack Jessica in a crowd, and even if she did, Jessica
was intelligent enough to fend her off for a
minute or two until he returned. Kaei did
not have a talent for getting herself out of
trouble.

Almost the instant he appeared, he found
himself on the defensive. A strike meant for
Kaei hit him hard, mostly because he was
unprepared. The mental blow had the dis-
tinct aura of a witch to it, so he quickly
turned his attention to the attacker.

He swore aloud as he recognized Dominique Vida. She had probably followed
Jessica here and run into Kaei on the way.
Kaei had had more than her share of arguments with witches.

Dominique fell back slightly into a stance of readiness, recognizing that she suddenly had a new, far more powerful foe.

Dominique was one of two vampire hunters who had ever won a fight against anyone in Aubrey's line. The other one he had dealt with accordingly. As for Dominique, no one had managed to get inside her guard sufficiently to plant a knife.

For a moment he was grateful Fala had taken his knife from him during their fight earlier. Dominique could have used it against him; her ancestors' magic had forged it.

Then Jessica returned to his thoughts. As much as he'd like to draw out this confrontation with such a worthy foe, he didn't have time to dally here with Dominique.

Instead, he did the only thing he could to get her out of the place.

He changed shape into the one he favored—a black wolf—and lunged, taking Dominique to the ground. She didn't expect him to be so reckless, which was the only reason her knife swiped across his stomach instead of plunging into his heart.

He clenched his teeth against the pain as the silver blade sliced his skin open. The wound was shallow, but the magic in the knife made it burn. He would likely have a scar.

Before the witch could recover, he used his mind to bring them both far away from New Mayhem. Then he rolled off her and sprinted, gaining as much distance as he could. Once he was far enough away that she could no longer latch on to his power and follow him, he disappeared, returning to Las Noches with a prayer that Jessica would still be there.

CHAPTER 27

JESSICA CUT THROUGH THE WOODS on her way back to Caryn and Hasana's house. A small river ran behind New Mayhem; it went through Red Rock Forest and eventually tapered off into Aqua Pond, which was close to the witches' home. She followed that river instead of taking the less direct route along the roads. As she had said to Aubrey, if anything wished to kill her, it would do so just as easily in the woods as on the road or anywhere else. She was too tired to take the long way.

At one point she paused to admire the full moon as it bounced and flickered on the river's surface. In the midst of that peaceful moment, someone grabbed her by the throat from behind.

"So the author would grace me with her presence." The mocking voice was one Jessica recognized instantly: Fala's. Jessica could feel the vampire's cool breath on the back of her neck; it sent a shiver down her spine.

"Leave me alone," Jessica said, her voice calm despite her fear. If Fala had decided to kill her, then she would not be swayed by groveling or cries for mercy. She would probably enjoy hearing them, but they wouldn't motivate her to do any less damage. Talking, at least, might buy time—time in which Fala might simply grow bored, or Aubrey might show up to beat her into a bloody pulp.

"Ha!" Fala exclaimed. "After all the trouble you've caused?"

Jessica had no time to answer; Fala shoved her, nearly sending her into the icy river. She turned back around in time to watch Fala approach.

"You human fool," Fala said, smirking. "You act so sure, so unafraid, so . . . *important*, as if you can't be killed just as easily as any other human. Just like your mother—"

"What do you know about my mother?" Jessica felt her anger rise at the reference, and again she saw Anne in her mind's eye—not killed by Fala's hand, but dead by her order nonetheless.

Fala's smirk widened. "About Raisa, you mean?" she asked sweetly. "About that poor, selfish half-wit Siete had us all practically baby-sitting for? I was there when she gave birth," Fala spat. "I would have killed you on the spot if Siete hadn't told me not to."

Jessica recoiled, the slow-boiling rage that was emanating from Fala, overshadowing even Jessica's surprise. So this was the reason for her hatred. Jessica knew Fala too well not to understand how she reacted to commands.

Once again Fala didn't give her time to respond, but instead disappeared. Jessica turned to search for her and felt a sharp tug on her hair. Fala was behind her again.

"Ever heard of fighting fair?" Jessica barked, grabbing the hand that was holding her hair, though it was strong as a steel clamp and not about to be forced open.

"Life isn't fair, and neither is death," Fala answered, yanking harder. As she did so, the tight grip forced Jessica's head back, baring her throat. "But I'll make it a bit more sporting. . . ."

Fala drew a knife that had been hidden in her tight clothing and flashed it in front of Jessica's face for a moment before she threw it across the clearing. Jessica couldn't see where it landed, but she heard the thump as it hit a tree. "Maybe I'll even give you a chance to retrieve it if I get bored, Jessie."

"Don't call me Jessie." It was an automatic reaction and was rewarded by another yank, and then a pain, sharp and strong, as Fala's teeth pierced the skin at her throat.

The pain faded quickly, replaced by a floating sensation as five thousand years of vampiric mind pressed against her own. Fala wrapped an arm around Jessica's waist, holding her in place as well as keeping her standing when she finally lost awareness of her body.

Jessica was weightless—sea foam on the back of a wave, or perhaps a feather carried by the breeze.

Then she recognized the trap, and a tendril of fear snaked into her mind. But the pain would begin only if she fought; she could simply stay here, resting—

Before she could let Fala's mind control

convince her otherwise, she drove an elbow back into the vampire's gut, at the same time slamming herself back to throw Fala into a tree behind them.

Fala let go with a hiss of rage, and Jessica hurried across the clearing, knowing Fala's injuries would stop her for no more than a few moments. She could feel a trickle of blood sliding down her neck and onto her black shirt, but the wound wasn't likely to be fatal. Fala hadn't had enough time.

Yet, she amended as she saw the cold fury in Fala's eyes.

"That's *it*," Fala hissed. "Do you seek death, Jessica? Or are you just fond of pain?" Each word was filled with venom. "I would have made this so much easier on you, but you chose to do it the hard way."

"I might die, but which one of us will hurt more tomorrow?" Jessica snapped before she could think better of it.

"I will be very sure you feel every drop of life as it leaves your veins," Fala threatened, her voice almost a whisper, "and that your body screams when it starts to starve from oxygen loss, and that you hear the silence when your heart finally stops."

She grabbed Jessica by the throat and

threw her almost casually into a tree. As Jessica's right shoulder slammed into the trunk, she gritted her teeth past the pain. The bone probably wasn't broken; Fala would do worse before this was over.

"I guess you know what you're describing," Jessica growled, her anger rising above her common sense. "From your days in that sandy, dirty cell where you were chained like the dog you are."

Fala was almost upon her. Jessica struck Fala's cheekbone with her closed fist, which fazed the vampire for only a second before she caught Jessica's wrist and tossed her into another tree. Jessica's hands and arms hit the tree first, absorbing some of the blow, but then she felt her head and bad shoulder strike the unyielding wood, and black spots danced in front of her eyes. She suspected this was her second concussion in as many days.

"Damn you, human!" Fala spat. "You aren't going to wake up. Your death will be your death. Do you understand? You are prey, and always will be. Mortal ... weak ... *prey.*"

Jessica stood painfully, trying to clear her vision. She had far too much pride to face

Fala like the feeble prey-beast the vampire saw her as.

"I know your talents at inflicting pain, Fala," she grumbled. "But even with them, you will never make me your prey."

CHAPTER 28

RAGE FLICKERED across Fala's face for a few seconds, until a lazy, dangerous smile grew to replace it.

Wise up, child, came Fala's voice, suddenly smooth and eerily civil. Jessica felt a moment of panic as she heard the voice in her mind — as she felt the words overlaying her own thoughts. Then the fear faded, and there was only the sound of the cool, unarguable voice.

I've read your writing, Fala continued calmly, and Jessica had no choice but to listen. *You know the difference between predator and prey. You were born human, and you will die human — prey and nothing more.*

As Fala stepped forward, Jessica moved

to meet her. Fala pulled Jessica's hair back yet again to bare her throat, and Jessica relaxed, allowing the vampire to do so. Fala was simply a higher race, and there was no arguing with the fact. By nature she was a predator.

And Jessica was just her prey. . . .

Prey?

That last thought didn't sit well. Instead, it brought crashing down the house of cards Fala had so easily erected in Jessica's mind.

Jessica shoved the vampire away with both arms, ignoring the screaming pain in her right shoulder as she did so.

"Get the hell out of my mind." She spat the words, a hoarse command, and Fala's expression went still, frozen in anger and disbelief. Jessica had slipped her mind control twice now.

"It seems to me that you were human once, Fala," Jessica continued, ignoring the blood that trickled from several of her wounds, and the black spots that bounced along the edge of her vision. "But I suppose you don't need to be reminded of *your* experiences as prey."

Fala's hand whipped forward and clamped over Jessica's throat, pressing her into a tree and cutting off her oxygen. "Watch your words, human. Unless you want me to squeeze your vertebrae straight through your windpipe."

Jessica couldn't answer as she struggled to breathe. Fala let go, throwing her to the ground hard enough to send splinters of pain through the arm she caught herself with.

"You picked the wrong person to fight, Jessica," Fala told her, pacing near her head. "Because I like pain—your pain—and I *really* like causing it."

"That's called sadism, and I think it's some kind of psychological disorder," Jessica grumbled, rolling onto her front so that she could use her left arm to push herself up.

Fala kicked her in the back of the head while she was still on her knees. "So are suicidal tendencies," she countered.

Black and red spots fought for domination in Jessica's mind as she felt herself being yanked to her feet by one of her injured arms. The world suddenly lost all focus, and she was dropped back to the ground.

"Pitiful," she heard Fala grunt.

Slowly, excruciatingly, Jessica forced herself to her feet as Fala walked away to lounge on the riverbank. Leaning against a tree for support, Jessica touched the back of her head and found it sticky with her own blood.

As soon as she felt capable of walking, Jessica scanned the clearing for the knife that Fala had thrown earlier. She spotted it partially embedded in a tree trunk nearby and staggered to it. She bit her lip to hold back a yelp of pain as she wrapped her hands around the knife's hilt and yanked it from the wood. Both her arms screamed at the effort.

She recognized the blade as Aubrey's and was surprised that Fala had managed to steal it from him. Though simple, it wasn't a knife one would mistake; the word *Fenris* was inscribed in the handle. Jessica knew the damage it could do to vampiric flesh, with all the poisonous magic burned deep into the silver of the blade by the vampire-slayer witch who had forged it. The knife felt almost alive in her hand, and she could feel its magic slither up her arm. Some of the pain dulled.

Never having handled a knife before as a weapon, she had no hope of fatally wounding Fala, but maybe she could hurt her enough that she would go away.

Jessica planted the knife loosely in the tree, a plan slowly forming in her mind.

"So, I see you're walking again," Fala sighed, appearing in front of her only seconds after Jessica had stepped away from the tree. "I must not have hit you hard enough."

Jessica backed up toward the knife, protecting her right arm. The wounded-bird routine was old but effective. Fala wouldn't consider the knife a threat because it would be impossible for Jessica to remove it one-handed, behind her back.

Fala stepped forward again, and Jessica felt behind her with her left arm as she backed up. Her hand was on the knife, but before she could do anything with it, Fala grabbed her again and dragged her forward.

Jessica's vision spun at the sudden movement, and the next instant she felt the sting as Fala's teeth pierced her throat once more.

This time, Fala made no effort to make it easy on her. The pain began instantly, not dulled by mind control or any hint of tenderness.

Though she had written about it many times, Jessica was not prepared. The pain in her head and her arms was nothing compared to the burning, suffocating sensation that now replaced those earlier annoyances. Despite her efforts not to, she heard her own voice shout out, a useless cry.

A wave of blackness spread across her vision, but she managed to fend it off as she yanked an arm free from Fala's grip.

Fala shifted a bit, and Jessica felt as if her skin had just been flayed from her body; she moaned in agony as her knees gave out under her, but somehow, just barely, she was able to grope for the knife.

She pulled the knife forward in an arc, and though she had no strength and no sight with which to aim, the blade glanced off Fala's side, slicing open the vampire's arm.

To a human, the wound would surely have been fatal. If Fala had been weaker, she too might have died. As it was, Jessica was certain it hurt like Hell.

Fala shrieked in rage and pain and hit Jessica, hard, on the left side of her chest. Jessica heard something snap and was knocked backward into the tree, hitting the wound on her head again.

Fala disappeared, cradling her arm against her chest. That was all Jessica saw before she sank into unconsciousness.

CHAPTER 29

FALA COULD SHIELD HER MIND too well for Aubrey to locate her, and neither Jager nor Moira would help him.

Only twenty minutes had passed since the tussle with Dominique, but he well knew the damage Fala could have done even that quickly. He had spent the time looking for Fala and berating himself for leaving Jessica alone, and little else. He hadn't even bothered to replace the shirt Dominique's knife had bloodied, but had simply tossed it in the trash somewhere.

Now Aubrey paced in Fala's room, waiting for her to return, all the while envisioning the new forms of pain he could introduce her to if she had killed Jessica.

When Fala finally did enter the room, she looked quite a bit worse for wear. Her arm had been sliced open, and blood was still dripping from the slowly healing wound. She was trembling, though Aubrey couldn't tell whether the cause was pain, chill, or rage.

"Damn both of you to Hell and back!" she growled when she saw him. "Get out of my room or I'll tear out your heart and feed it to Ahemait myself."

Judging by her mood, she might very well try. Ahemait was the Egyptian devourer of the dead. When Fala brought up the mythology of her human background, she was best avoided.

Instead, Aubrey's anger responded to hers.

He slammed her against the wall, his hand around her throat, and heard the crunch as her windpipe broke. The injury would heal quickly, but he could tell that, despite her high tolerance for it, Fala did not appreciate the pain.

She threw a bolt of her power at him and he stumbled back a step. Dodging quickly, he barely avoided his own knife when she threw it at him. The blade stuck in the wall.

"What did you do to her?" he demanded.

"Only what *you* should have done a week ago!" Fala snapped.

This time it was Fala's turn to stumble as Aubrey lashed out, his anger making the blow even harder. "Where is she?" he said quietly, his voice cold.

Fala laughed. "You honestly expect me to tell you?"

Meeting her gaze, Aubrey paused before answering. He saw her expression change as she recognized the complete, smoldering rage in his eyes. "Yes."

"She's somewhere on the river," Fala spat, wise enough to recognize that fighting him at this moment was a dangerous idea. "I hope the crows have gotten to her by now."

Aubrey disappeared, bringing himself to the edge of New Mayhem, where the river passed by.

Once again he changed himself into a wolf, a creature that could move faster and more surely through the woods. Following the river, he covered a mile in only a few minutes. Finally, less than two miles from New Mayhem, in the thick of the forest, he caught Jessica's scent and brought himself instantly to her side.

Jessica was pasty white, her breathing was wet and shallow, and her heart alternated between racing and threatening to stop.

She was alive, but not for long, and he knew no way to help her. Three thousand years of killing had taught him nothing about undoing this kind of damage.

After a moment of hesitation in which he swallowed his pride, he left Jessica's side and brought himself to the home of Hasana and Caryn Smoke. He could sense Caryn's magic, stronger than her mother's, even outside the house.

Had he not killed all his gods long ago, Aubrey would have prayed that Caryn would be willing to help. Anxiously he brought himself to her side.

CHAPTER 30

CARYN HAD NEARLY FAINTED from fright when Aubrey first appeared in her room, but his rapid explanation had shoved all personal concerns out of the way, making room for the disciplined healer to come forth. She had been working now for nearly an hour.

She was from the oldest known line of healers on Earth, but even her abilities had limits.

She felt weak from fatigue. Her clothing was soaking wet from when she had accidentally fallen in the river, and her heart was beating twice as fast as normal. Her face was stained with worried tears as she chanted and held her left hand, palm down, over

Jessica's heart, channeling much-needed energy into the dying girl. Her other hand was constantly moving—soothing Jessica's brow, holding her hand, or drawing power from the earth.

Jessica's heart had been beating evenly for several minutes, but now it skipped once and Caryn gasped in pain, her chant stopping.

"I can't do this." Fresh tears rolled down her face.

"Should I get Hasana?" Aubrey suggested. "Maybe she—"

"She won't," Caryn interrupted, remembering her mother's anger when Jessica had left the house the day before. "She hates your kind and calls Jessica a traitor to the human race. Monica would have helped; she could have done it. But I just *can't*. I can't save her, and I could kill myself trying."

"Is there anyone else?" Aubrey asked, sounding frantic.

"Vida would kill her," Caryn answered, "and Light's dead." She cast Aubrey a sharp glance, knowing that his kind had murdered Lila, the last in the Light line. "All the others are too weak. Whoever did this broke one of her ribs, and now there's blood in one of her lungs; she's going to start drowning in it soon. Besides that, she's just about drained. It's amazing I can even keep her heart beating at all. Plus, she's got at least a dozen other injuries . . . I don't know of anything in science or magic that can heal her."

Caryn looked beseechingly at Aubrey, hoping he knew something she did not.

He knew nothing she wanted to hear. "I can kill—I can't heal," he sighed.

"I've been channeling my own . . . I don't know what to call it . . . *life* into her, but if I keep doing it we're *both* going to die. No witch short of an Arun could survive this, and they're part vampire . . ."

Caryn trailed off, defeated.

"I could."

She looked at Aubrey blankly for a moment after he spoke those words.

"Unless Fala decided to tear her heart out, her injuries are really rather insignificant to my kind," he clarified.

Finally Caryn understood. She had channeled from other witches in the past. If she could take energy from a vampire and give it to Jessica . . . would that heal her?

It might.

"I could kill you accidentally," she warned him.

"I've lived a long time."

"This is very definitely going to get me disowned," she muttered, hoping her mother would find some way to forgive her. "I need you on my right," she told Aubrey.

After he had shifted position, Caryn placed her right hand just above Jessica's heart, one of the three strongest energy centers. For healing, the heart center was best.

There were no words to accurately describe what she did next. Her own energy centers were open, forming a path from Aubrey to Jessica, and now as she tapped into Aubrey's —

She gasped as the power flowed through her. That was all it could possibly be called. Not life, not *chi* as Hasana called it or simply energy as Monica had taught her, but pure, unrestricted *power.* No wonder his mind was so strong . . .

Caryn forced herself to control the power, which required all her years of practice, and then focused on channeling it into Jessica.

Jessica's own aura was strong, and Caryn wasn't surprised to note vampiric traces in it. She directed Aubrey's power to the areas of Jessica's injuries, where the girl's aura was weakest.

First she focused on the crack in Jessica's skull. It knitted itself together within seconds, and the blood that had pooled inside was reabsorbed into the veins as they repaired themselves.

The lung came next. The organ collapsed into itself and then regrew—small like a child's at first, but quickly expanding to full size. The rib mended in moments.

The rest of Jessica's body healed just as quickly, simply from the overflow of power. Caryn was grateful, since she was becoming sleepy. How could she be so exhausted with all this power running through her?

She was trying very hard not to think about what this process was going to do to her. She knew only one story that involved channeling the vampiric aura: Midnight Smoke, mother of Ardiente Arun, had drawn the vampiric aura into herself to save a human from becoming one of them. Since then, all Midnight's ancestors had carried a vampiric taint. Ardiente and Midnight had split from the line they had been born in and become the first in the Arun line. Caryn was descended from their relations, who had continued the Smoke line.

Caryn was feeling light-headed. There was nothing more she could do for Jessica; if this wasn't enough, then nothing would have worked. She quickly closed off Aubrey's power centers, then her own, aware that if she passed out before doing so she would probably kill all three of them.

With her eyes closed, she focused on Jessica yet again, trying to ascertain what still needed to be done.

While most of her body had healed, Jessica was still all too human. The newly healed areas needed the support of more blood than she had. Fala had taken too much.

"We should get her to a hospital, or she's still going to die," Caryn said, her voice uneven. "She needs blood."

For a moment Aubrey looked up, and his black eyes held no warmth as they focused on Caryn and then fell to her throat. She could see the effort as he turned his head away.

He was no longer the perfect, drop-dead-gorgeous immortal he had been. He was paler than ever, and his eyes were unfocused. He looked as if he had been drained as surely as Jessica had. Of course, when it came to his kind, power and blood were often all but interchangeable.

Caryn lay down as another wave of fatigue washed over her, and watched silently as Aubrey tried to rouse Jessica.

CHAPTER 31

JESSICA COULD BARELY BREATHE past the pain in her chest. Every muscle in her body had cramped, and she was shivering with cold.

Jessica! She recognized Aubrey's voice in her mind, though she had never heard him sound so distraught.

Slowly she dragged herself into the waking world.

No, not dead . . . I wouldn't hurt so much if I was dead, she thought absently. It was difficult to form a coherent sentence.

Aubrey pulled her attention back to him. *Not dead yet,* he said quickly, bluntly. *But you will be soon if we don't do something.* He paused, shaking her a bit to keep her attention from drifting away.

Careful. I'm not sure that arm is still fully attached, she answered, her wry humor returning to her.

I can bring you to a hospital, and they can give you blood. There's probably still time, he told her. *Or if you want it — I know you said before that you did — I can give you mine.*

If she'd had the breath to do so, she would have laughed.

Did she want to be a vampire? To stay in New Mayhem, in the community that had been her life for years; to be with Aubrey, the only one she'd ever felt completely at ease with; to never be prey again?

Then there was also the bonus of immortality, and the tempting idea of pummeling Fala into a bloody smear on the wall.

You need to ask? she finally said, and heard Aubrey sigh with relief.

Of course, she would be the first of his line — *her* line, she amended, realizing she'd soon be a part of it — to have been asked. They had been changed for various reasons — on a whim, out of spite or hatred or love. But not one of them had had a choice in the matter.

Jessica smiled wryly as she realized the favor that Fala had unintentionally given. Jessica had fought for her life when Fala had taken her blood, and now had free choice as Aubrey offered his.

Aubrey drew his knife—the same one he had used to shed Ather's blood years ago, when he had been changed. He slid the blade across his skin at the base of his throat, and he pulled Jessica toward him to drink.

She had known this moment in the lives of each of her vampiric characters; had described it in words and tasted it in dreams. But never had she fully understood it.

As she drank, she closed her eyes and abandoned herself to the sweet taste and the feeling that came with it. The English language had no way to properly express this rolling power that filled her like blue lightning, slipping into every molecule of her body and changing everything it touched.

Jessica tried to cling to the sensation, but a gentle numbness began to ease across her skin and into her mind, like the first tendrils of sleep. She was only vaguely aware of the fact that her heart had slowed and stopped, and only distantly did she realize that she was no longer breathing. The inevitable blackness of death stole over her, and she succumbed to it willingly, trusting that she would wake shortly.

Jazlyn was in constant pain for the first few days, but even that pain served as a welcome reminder that she was alive.

The first thing she did was go to the church, inside which she had not dared set foot since the day she had been changed. The priest blessed her and listened to her confession, which she abridged for the sake of his sanity.

She thought she had been given another chance — a chance to leave behind the life of darkness and evil. When the child came — Carl's child, whom she should have had years before — she thought it was a sign that she'd been forgiven.

Instead, the child was a reminder of her past. Jessica was flawless, brilliant . . . and shadowed by the night. She looked nothing like Carl or Jazlyn; instead, she had Siete's fair skin, black hair, and emerald eyes.

Those eyes could look upon someone and see the darkest parts of their soul.

Jessica had spent more than twenty years in Jazlyn's womb, kept alive only by Siete's blood. She was more his child than Jazlyn's.

There was no way for Jazlyn to raise the child

*who brought back her every painful memory. No
child deserved to have a mother who could not brush
her raven hair, or look into her gemstone eyes,
without shuddering.*

*Jazlyn put the child up for adoption, so that she
could be given to caring parents who knew only of
sunlight and laughter. Jessica deserved that life;
she had done nothing wrong.*

*Jazlyn prayed that her child would never be
touched by the darkness of her past.*

CHAPTER 32

JESSICA'S HEART HAD STOPPED. Her face was almost white, and as cool as the fall air surrounding her. She had died only moments before, as Aubrey's blood had entered her system. He left her side reluctantly to check on Caryn.

Caryn's breathing was slow and deep, and she seemed to be fine except for the cataleptic sleep she was in. At the moment Aubrey's hunger was more of a danger to the witch than anything else.

Almost without thinking, he brought both girls and himself to his seldom-used house in New Mayhem, where no one would bother them. The forest had far too many predators in it to leave them alone there, and he didn't know what Caryn would want him to tell her mother.

He put Caryn in the one bedroom with windows, knowing that no witch would want to wake and not be able to see either the stars or the sun. But he left Jessica in a bedroom with heavy blackout curtains that would block the sun while she slept.

Then, before the mingled scents of Jessica's and Caryn's blood could defeat his usually iron self-control, he went searching for dinner. Having fed well, he returned home to watch over the girls, and finally allowed his mind to turn to other things.

Like how many ways he could fillet Fala, for one. Or how many ways he *would* fillet Fala, for two.

An hour before sunset, Aubrey dragged himself away from Jessica's side. Fala needed to be dealt with before Jessica woke.

He appeared just behind Fala in her room, his knife at her throat and his mind clamped on hers to hold her in place.

"I hope she sliced you open *very* well," he snarled, pressing the edge of the blade into her throat just slightly.

"And I hope she's very, *very* dead," Fala answered in kind, softly so as to not put any more pressure against the blade. Despite her caution, a thin line of blood appeared on her dark Egyptian skin. "If she isn't, I'll correct that error soon."

"I suggest you don't," he said. Considering how the last fight had gone, Jessica might win if Fala chose to pick another.

"She drew blood, Aubrey," Fala answered. "I have claim, and you can't stop me from acting on it."

What he had done for Jessica would have been illegal had Fala conquered her pride earlier and admitted that Jessica had been the one who wounded her. Instead, she had waited until now to actually call on blood claim, and now was too late.

"The law only applies if she's human," he answered coldly.

Then his attention was drawn away as he sensed a familiar presence just outside the door.

Jessica had washed the blood off her skin, but her pallor showed that she still needed to feed.

"Don't stop her," Jessica said. Aubrey released Fala but didn't move away; Jessica was certainly not strong enough to best Fala in a fight now, before she had even fed. Yet she walked calmly toward Fala, looking at the vampire with scorn. "Wounded by a human . . . what a blow that must have been to your pride."

Fala growled, but she restrained herself from attacking with Aubrey so near.

"I have no desire to fight you," Jessica said simply, almost regally.

Fala's eyes narrowed in response, but she made no immediate comment. Aubrey knew that Fala could tell as well as he could how strong Jessica would be once she had fed.

"However," Jessica continued, just as controlled, "if you ever harm anyone I care about, or come anywhere near me, you will very quickly learn just how many interesting stories about your past I still have to share."

She didn't wait for Fala to react. Instead, she disappeared, presumably to feed.

CHAPTER 33

JESSICA RETURNED SHORTLY to Aubrey's home in New Mayhem, her fair skin flushed with the blood meal she had taken in a sleazy corner of New York City only minutes before.

Aubrey was lounging on one of the couches in the living room when she entered. He stood and approached her. "Caryn went home, but she left this for you," he said, handing her a letter.

Jessica scanned Caryn's letter — a long, rambling, maudlin farewell. She made a point to hide her own emotions as she silently said her goodbyes to the person who had probably been her last tie to the mortal world.

"And," Aubrey added reluctantly, glancing toward the table, where Jessica's computer now sat, "she had me bring that here."

Jessica smiled wickedly. How harmless the contraption appeared—plain black plastic without a single scratch or mark to show how much tumult it had helped her cause. She wandered to the table and brushed the laptop's case affectionately.

Aubrey had followed her. "Do you really need that?" he asked.

"I can't write without it," she answered, assuming the closest she could manage to an innocent expression before the underlying mischief showed through.

"You live to make trouble, don't you?"

"Life is nothing without a little chaos to make it interesting." She turned to face him and playfully raised her gaze to meet his, challenging. "What do you want to do about it?"

Don't miss *Shattered Mirror*
by **Amelia Atwater-Rhodes**

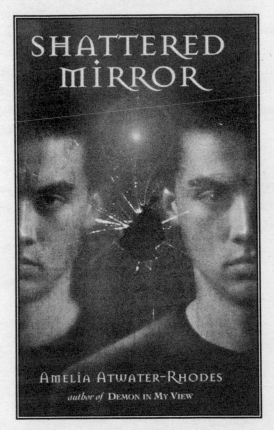

SHATTERED
MIRROR

AMELIA ATWATER-RHODES

author of DEMON IN MY VIEW

0-385-32793-5

Excerpt from *Shattered Mirror*
by Amelia Atwater-Rhodes
Copyright © 2001 by Amelia Atwater-Rhodes

Published by Delacorte Press
an imprint of Random House Children's Books
a division of Random House, Inc.
1540 Broadway
New York, New York 10036

Reprinted by arrangement with Delacorte Press

SEVEN THIRTY-FIVE is a beastly hour to begin school, Sarah thought, as she opened her locker. The bell rang and she sighed. Hopefully being the new girl would excuse her tardiness. It certainly had no other perks. She thought fleetingly of the hunting companions she had left behind, with whom she had crashed bashes and stalked the darkest corners of the city. By morning, rarely had a blade been left clean.

She forcibly banished such thoughts. She was here now, and it was time to begin this new life.

Her first block was American history, and

though she located it easily, the class had already begun when she slipped through the door.

"Sarah Green?" the teacher confirmed as Sarah turned over the folded pink pass from the office. Mr. Smith was a balding, tired-looking man, whose crisp suit pants and shirt seemed out of place in the high school. He gestured toward the class. "Take a seat . . . there's one open right next to Robert—"

"Actually, someone's sitting there," one of the boys in the back of the room called. As Sarah's attention turned to Robert, she realized that he looked vaguely familiar, but she couldn't place his face in her memory. He had looked up just long enough to see who had come in the door, and was now writing something in a notebook. The desk next to him appeared empty to Sarah, the chair was vacant.

Mr. Smith looked surprised, but he skimmed the class again.

"There's a seat here," someone else called, and Sarah glanced to see who had spoken.

Black hair, fair skin, *black* eyes. Vampire. She recognized him instantly, but Mr. Smith was already hustling her toward the empty seat.

The aura of the vampire beside her was so faint that her skin wasn't even tingling. He was either very young, or very weak, and she could tell that he did not feed on human prey. Probably SingleEarth, harmless as Caryn had said. There was a female vampire in the class as well. She looked almost as weak, and although her aura showed a hint of human blood—probably from one of the plethora of humans at SingleEarth willing to bare their throats—it was obvious she did not kill when she hunted. Neither of them would be able to sense Sarah's aura, so unless they knew her by sight, they would likely assume that she was just another human.

"Christopher Ravena," the leech said, introducing himself as she slid into her chair. He nodded across the class. "That's my sister, Nissa." The girl he had gestured to waved slightly. Though her hair was a shade lighter, the resemblance between the siblings was marked—including the mild vampiric aura.

"Nice to meet you," she answered politely, though inside she grimaced. *This could be a very long year.*